THE
ORANGE GROVE

THE
ORANGE GROVE

LARRY TREMBLAY

Translated from the French
by Sheila Fischman

milkweed
editions

The characters and events in this book are fictitious. Any similarity to real persons, living or dead, is coincidental and not intended by the author.

Published 2016 by Milkweed Editions
Printed in Canada
Cover design by Gretchen Achilles
Cover photo by Jose-Luis Saez Martinez / EyeEm / Getty Images
Author photo by Bernard Préfontaine
16 17 18 19 20   5 4 3 2 1
First US Edition

Milkweed Editions, an independent nonprofit publisher, gratefully acknowledges sustaining support from the Jerome Foundation; the Lindquist & Vennum Foundation; the McKnight Foundation; the National Endowment for the Arts; the Target Foundation; and other generous contributions from foundations, corporations, and individuals. Also, this activity is made possible by the voters of Minnesota through a Minnesota State Arts Board Operating Support grant, thanks to a legislative appropriation from the arts and cultural heritage fund, and a grant from the Wells Fargo Foundation Minnesota. For a full listing of Milkweed Editions supporters, please visit www.milkweed.org.

Library of Congress Cataloging-in-Publication Data

Tremblay, Larry, 1954- author. | Fischman, Sheila, translator.
The orange grove : a novel / Larry Tremblay ; translated from the French by Sheila Fischman.
Other titles: Orangeraie. English
Description: First edition. | Minneapolis : Milkweed Editions, 2016.
Identifiers: LCCN 2015050417 (print) | LCCN 2015050908 (ebook) | ISBN 9781571311191 (paperback) | ISBN 9781571319340 (e-book)
Subjects: LCSH: Twin brothers—Fiction. | War—Psychological aspects—Fiction. | BISAC: FICTION / Literary. | FICTION / Political. | FICTION / Coming of Age. | FICTION / Family Life.
Classification: LCC PQ3919.2.T7187 O7313 2016 (print) | LCC PQ3919.2.T7187 (ebook) | DDC 843/.914--dc23
LC record available at http://lccn.loc.gov/2015050417

Milkweed Editions is committed to ecological stewardship. We strive to align our book production practices with this principle, and to reduce the impact of our operations in the environment. We are a member of the Green Press Initiative, a nonprofit coalition of publishers, manufacturers, and authors working to protect the world's endangered forests and conserve natural resources. *The Orange Grove* was printed on acid-free 100% postconsumer-waste paper by Friesens Corporation.

For Joan

CONTENTS

AMED

If Amed cried, Aziz cried too. If Aziz laughed, Amed laughed too. People would make fun of them, saying: "Later on they'll marry each other."

Their grandmother's name was Shahina. With her bad eyes she always confused them. She would call them her two drops of water in the desert. "Stop holding hands," she would say, "I feel as if I'm seeing double." Or, "Some day, there won't be any more drops, there will be water, that's all." She could have said: "One day there will be blood. That's all."

Amed and Aziz found their grandparents in the ruins of their house. Their grandmother's skull had been smashed in by a beam. Their grandfather was lying in his bedroom, his body shredded by the bomb that had come from the side of the mountain where every night the sun disappeared.

It had still been night when the bomb fell. But Shahina had already been up. Her body was found in the kitchen.

"What was she doing in the kitchen in the middle of the night?" asked Amed.

"We'll never know. Maybe she was baking a cake in secret," his mother replied.

"Why in secret?" asked Aziz.

"Maybe for a surprise," Tamara suggested to her two sons, sweeping the air with her hand as if brushing away a fly.

Their grandmother used to talk to herself. In fact, she had liked to talk to everything around her. The boys had seen her ask questions of the flowers in the garden, argue with the stream that ran between their houses. She could spend hours bent over the water, whispering to it. Zahed had been ashamed to see his mother behave in this way. He had rebuked her for setting a bad example for her grandsons. "You act like a lunatic," he'd yelled. Shahina had bowed her head and closed her eyes, in silence.

One day Amed had told his grandmother:

"There's a voice in my head. It talks to itself. I can't make it be quiet, it says strange things. As if someone else were hidden inside me, someone bigger than me."

"Tell me, Amed, tell me the strange things it says to you."

"I can't tell you because I forget them right away."

That had been a lie. He did not forget them.

Aziz had been to the big city once. His father, Zahed, rented a car. Hired a chauffeur. They left at dawn. Aziz watched the new landscape file past the car window. Thought the space the car sliced through was beautiful. Thought the trees disappearing from sight beautiful. Thought the cows, horns smeared with red, beautiful, calm as big stones on the burning ground. The road was shaken by joy and anger. Aziz was writhing in pain. And smiling. His gaze drowned the landscape with tears. And the landscape was like the image of a country.

Zahed had said to his wife:

"I'm taking him to the hospital in the big city."

"I will pray, Amed will pray" was Tamara's simple reply.

When the driver announced they were finally approaching the city, Aziz fainted and saw nothing of the splendors he'd heard about. He regained consciousness lying in a bed. In the room were other beds, with other children in them. He thought he was lying in all those beds. He thought the excessive pain had multiplied his body. He thought he was twisting in pain in all those beds with all those bodies. A doctor was leaning over him. Aziz smelled his spicy perfume. The doctor was smiling at Aziz. Even so, Aziz was afraid of the man.

"Did you sleep well?"

Aziz said nothing. The doctor straightened up, his smile faded. He talked to Aziz's father. Father and doctor exited the big room. Zahed's fists were clenched. He was breathing heavily.

A few days later, Aziz was feeling better. They gave him a thick liquid to drink. He took it morning and night. It was pink. He didn't like the taste, but it relieved his pain. His father came to see him every day. Said he was staying with his cousin Kacir. That was all he said. Zahed looked at Aziz in silence, touched his brow. His hand was as hard as a branch. Once, Aziz woke with a start. His father was looking at him, sitting on a chair. His gaze frightened Aziz.

A little girl was in the bed next to that of Aziz. Her name was Naliffa. She told Aziz that her heart had not grown properly in her chest.

"My heart grew upside down, you know, it's pointed the wrong way."

She said that to all the other children sleeping in the big hospital room. Naliffa talked to everybody. One night, Aziz screamed in his sleep. Naliffa was frightened. At daybreak, she told him what she'd seen.

"Your eyes went white like balls of dough, you stood up on your bed, and you waved your arms. I thought you were trying to scare me. I called to you. But your mind was no longer in your head. It had disappeared I don't know where. The nurses came. They put a screen around your bed."

"I had a nightmare."

"Why are there nightmares? Do you know?"

"I don't know, Naliffa. Mama often says, 'God only knows.'"

"Mama says the same thing: 'God only knows.' She also says, 'It's been that way since the dawn of time." The dawn of time, Mama told me, is the first night of the world. It was so dark that the first ray of sunlight that broke through the night howled in pain."

"More likely it was the night that howled as it was being pierced."

"Maybe," said Naliffa, "maybe."

A few days later, Zahed asked Aziz about the little girl who had been in the next bed. Aziz replied that her mother had come to get her because she was cured. His father lowered his head. He said nothing. After a long while, he raised his head again. He still didn't say anything. Then he bent over his son. He placed a kiss on his brow. It was the first time he'd done that. Aziz had tears in his eyes. His father murmured, "Tomorrow, we're going home too."

Aziz left with his father and the same driver. He watched the road fly past in the rearview mirror. His father was creating a strange silence, smoking in the car. He had brought dates and a cake. Before arriving at the house, Aziz asked his father if he was all better.

"You won't go back to the hospital again! Our prayers have been answered."

Zahed placed his big hand on his son's head. Aziz was happy. Three days later the bomb from the other side of the mountain split the night and killed his grandparents.

On the day Zahed and Aziz came back from the big city, Tamara received a letter from her sister, Dalimah. She had gone to America some years earlier for an internship in data processing. She had been selected from a hundred candidates, quite an achievement. But she'd never come back. Dalimah wrote regularly to her sister even though Tamara rarely replied. In the letters she described her life. There was no war over there, that was what made her so happy. And so daring. She offered to send money but Tamara curtly refused her help.

In her letter, Dalimah announced that she was pregnant. Her first child. She asked Tamara to come over with the twins. She would find a way to bring them to America. She let it be understood that Tamara should abandon Zahed. Leave him alone with his war and his groves of orange trees.

"How she's changed in a few years!"

There were days when Tamara hated her sister. She was mad at her: how could she expect Tamara to leave her husband? She wouldn't leave Zahed. No. And she would fight too, even if Dalimah wrote that their war was pointless, that there would only be losers.

Zahed had stopped asking for news about her long ago. For him, Dalimah was dead. He wouldn't even touch her letters. "I don't want to be soiled," he would say, disgusted. Dalimah's husband was an engineer. Dalimah never mentioned him in her letters. She knew that in her family's eyes he was a hypocrite and a coward. Like the bomb, he'd come from the other side of the mountain. He was an enemy. He'd fled to America. To gain acceptance there he had recounted horrors and lies about their people. That was what Tamara and Zahed believed. Had Dalimah not found anything better to do when she arrived there than to marry an enemy? How could she? "It was God who put him in my way," she had written to them one day. "She's an idiot," thought Tamara. "America has clouded her judgment. What is she waiting for? For us all to be slaughtered by her husband's friends? What did she think when she married him? That she was going to contribute to the peace process? Basically, she has always been selfish. Why bother telling her about our hardships? Who knows? Her husband might be thrilled."

Later, in a brief reply to her sister, Tamara said nothing about Aziz having been in the hospital. Or about the bomb that had just killed her parents-in-law.

Men pulled up in a jeep. Amed and Aziz caught sight of a cloud of dust on the road that ran close to their house. The family was in the orange grove. That was where Zahed had wanted to bury his parents. He had just thrown in the last spadeful of earth. His forehead and arms were wet with sweat. Tamara was crying and biting the inside of her cheek. The jeep stopped on the side of the road. Three men emerged from it. The tallest held a machine gun. They did not head for the orange grove immediately. They lit cigarettes. Amed dropped his brother's hand and went to the road. He wanted to hear what the three men were saying. He couldn't. They were speaking too quietly. The youngest of the three finally took a few steps towards him. Amed recognized Halim. He'd grown a lot.

"Remember me? I'm Halim. I met you at the village school. When there still was a school." Halim started to laugh.

"Yes, I remember you, you were the only one of the grown-ups who talked to my brother and me. Your beard's grown."

"We want to talk to your father, Zahed."

Amed headed for the orange grove, followed by the three men. His father approached them. Amed saw his mother's eyes harden. She shouted at him to join her. The men argued with Zahed for a long time. Tamara thought to herself that there was a curse on this day. She watched her husband. Zahed hung his head, looked at the ground. Halim gestured to Amed, who broke away from the arms of his mother, who was holding her two sons against her belly, to join the group of men. Zahed laid his hand on the boy's head, saying proudly:

"This is my son Amed."

"And the other boy?"

"Aziz, his twin brother."

They stayed till evening. Zahed showed them the ruins of his parents' house. They all looked up toward the mountain as if they were seeking in the sky the track of the bomb. Tamara made tea. She sent the children to their room. Later, Amed and Aziz watched out the window as the man with the machine gun went back to the jeep and returned a few minutes later, carrying a bag. They thought they heard their mother cry. Then the men left. The sound of the jeep driving away echoed in the night for a long time. Amed hugged his brother tight and finally fell asleep.

The next day Aziz said:

"Didn't you notice? The sounds don't sound the same and silence seems to be hiding to work on some dirty trick."

"You were sick. That's why you're imagining things."

But Amed knew that his brother was right. From his bedroom window he caught a glimpse of his mother. He called to her. She moved away. Amed thought she was crying. He saw her disappear behind the amaryllis his grandmother had planted the year before. Now they were enormous. Their open blossoms swallowed the light. Amed and Aziz went down to the first floor. Their mother hadn't fixed the morning meal. Their father hadn't slept, they could tell by his tired face. He was sitting on the kitchen floor. What was he doing there, alone? It was the first time the boys had seen their father doing that.

"Are you hungry?"

"No."

They were hungry though. Next to their father was a canvas bag.

"What's that?" asked Aziz. "Did the men in the jeep forget it?"

"They didn't forget it," said Zahed.

He gestured to his sons to sit beside him. Then he talked about the man with the machine gun.

"He's an important man," he told his sons. "He comes from the next village. His name is Soulayed. He talked to me with his heart. He insisted on seeing the ruins of your grandparents' house. He will pray for the salvation of their souls. He's a pious man. An educated man. When he finished drinking his tea he took my hand.

"He said to me: 'How peaceful your house is! I close my eyes and the perfume of the orange trees sweeps over me. Your father, Mounir, worked his whole life on this arid soil. It was the desert here. With God's help your father worked a miracle. Made oranges grow where there had been only sand and stones. Don't think that because I come to you with a machine gun, I don't have the eyes and ears of a poet. I hear and I see that which is just and pleasant. You are a bighearted man. Your house is clean. Everything in its place. Your wife's tea is delicious. You know what they say, too much sugar, too little sugar: good tea falls between the two. Your wife's is the golden mean. The stream that runs between your father's house and your own is in the very middle too. From the road it's the first thing one notices, the beauty that's exactly in the middle. Zahed, your father was known throughout the land. He was a just man. It took a just man to transform this faceless territory into a paradise. The birds are never wrong where paradise is concerned, even when they hide in the shadow of the mountains. They recognize it very quickly. Tell me, Zahed, do you know the names of the birds that are singing right now? Surely not. There are too many and their songs are too elusive. Through the window I can see some with wings that flash a saffron color. Those birds have come from very far away. Just now their vivid colors mingle with those of the orange grove where you have just buried your parents. And their song rings out like a blessing. But can these nameless birds lessen your grief? No. Revenge is the only answer for your grief. Listen carefully, Zahed. In nearby villages other houses have been destroyed. Many people have died because of missiles and bombs. Our enemies want to seize our land. They want our land to build their houses and make their wives pregnant. After invading our villages they will advance to the big city. They will kill our women. Enslave our children. And that will be the end of our country. Our earth will be soiled by their steps, by their spittle. Do you believe that God will allow this sacrilege? Do you believe that, Zahed?'

"That is what Soulayed said to your father."

Amed and Aziz dared not move or speak. Never had their father talked at such length. Zahed stood up. Took a few steps in the room.

Amed whispered to his brother: "He's thinking. When he walks like that it means he's thinking."

After a long moment Zahed opened the bag the men had left behind. Inside was a strange belt which he unrolled. It was so heavy he needed both hands to lift it.

"Soulayed brought it," Zahed told his sons. "At first I didn't realize what he was showing me. Halim put the belt on. That was when I understood that those men were here to see me. Your mother came in. She was bringing more tea. She saw Halim and started to shriek. She spilled the tray. The teapot fell to the floor. A glass broke. I asked your mother to pick it all up and come back with more tea. I apologized to Soulayed. Your mother shouldn't have shrieked."

Aziz wanted to touch the belt. His father pushed him away. He put it back in the bag and left the room. Amed and Aziz watched at the window as he disappeared in the fields of orange trees.

Tamara rarely talked with her husband. She preferred their silences to their usual arguments. They loved one another as men and women should love one another in the eyes of God and men.

Often, before joining her husband in bed, she would go into the garden. She would sit on the bench in front of the roses and inhale the rich scents that rose from the damp earth. Let herself be lulled by the music of insects, raise her head to seek the moon. Look at it as if it were an old friend she'd just run into. Some nights the moon made her think of a fingernail print in the flesh of the sky. She liked these moments when she was alone before infinity. Her children were sleeping. Her husband was waiting for her in their bedroom and she might have existed as a star that shone for worlds unknown. Gazing at the sky, Tamara wondered if the moon had known the desire for death, to disappear from the face of night and leave men orphans of the light. Its weak light borrowed from the sun's.

Beneath the starry sky, Tamara didn't fear talking to God. She felt as if she knew Him better than did her husband. Her words were lost in the sound of water in the stream. Yet she still hoped that they rose up to Him.

When the men who'd come in the jeep left their house, Zahed had insisted on giving them oranges and asked his wife to help him fill two big baskets. She'd refused. That night Tamara had spent longer than usual on the bench. She'd dared not utter the words that were burning her tongue. This time, too, her prayer remained silent:

"Your name is great, my heart too small to contain it entirely. What would You do with the prayer of a woman like me? My lips scarcely touch the shadow of Your first syllable. But they say that Your heart is greater than Your name. Your heart, no matter its size, is great enough that a woman can hear it in her own. That's what they say when talking about You and they speak only the truth. But why must one live in a country where time cannot do its work? The paint hasn't had time to peel nor the curtains to turn yellow, the plates haven't had time to chip. Things never serve their time, the living are always slower than the dead. Our men age faster than their wives. They dry like tobacco leaves. It's hatred that keeps their bones in place. Without hatred they would collapse and never get up again. The wind would make them disappear. All that would remain is the moaning of their wives in the night. Listen to me, I have two sons. One is the hand, the other the fist. One takes, the other gives. One day it's the one, another day the other. I beg you, don't take them both from me."

That was Tamara's prayer the night she refused to fill the two baskets with oranges.

After the village school was destroyed by bombs, Tamara turned herself into a teacher. Every morning she sat the two boys down in the kitchen next to the fat pots with blackened necks, and took great pleasure in her new role. There was talk of relocating the school, but no one in the village could agree on where. For months, then, families carried on as best they could. Amed and Aziz didn't complain. They liked being there in the fragrant kitchen, where bouquets of fresh mint hung from the ceiling along with strings of garlic. They even made progress. Amed's writing improved, and Aziz, despite his hospitalization, took to his multiplication tables with greater confidence.

As the boys were out of books, one morning Tamara thought to make notebooks out of leftover wrapping paper, and they, little kitchen scribblers, blackened the creased pages of these odd volumes with their stories. The boys took to the game right away. Amed even invented a character who embarked on impossible adventures. He explored distant planets, dug tunnels in the desert, struck down undersea creatures. Amed called him Dôdi, and endowed him with two mouths, one very little and one very big. Dôdi used his little mouth to communicate with insects and microbes. He used his big mouth to strike fear into the monsters he battled. But Dôdi sometimes spoke with his two mouths at the same time. Then the words he pronounced were comically deformed, creating new words and jumbled sentences that made the little apprentice writers laugh. Tamara took enormous pleasure in this. But after the night of the bombing and the death of their grandparents, those makeshift notebooks told only sad and cruel stories. And Dôdi went silent.

A week after the visit of the men in the jeep, the distant voice of Zahed came to Amed and Aziz in the kitchen, where they were working, without much enthusiasm, at their notebooks. He was calling them from the orange grove, where he spent twelve hours a day pruning, watering, and checking every tree. But this wasn't the hour when he stopped to rest. Amed and Aziz dropped their pencils and ran to join their father, anxious to know what he wanted. Tamara left the house. Zahed gestured for her to come as well. She shook her head and went back inside. Zahed insulted her in front of her sons, something he'd never done before. Amed and Aziz no longer recognized their father. And yet when he began to speak, his voice was calmer than usual.

"Observe, my sons, the purity of the light," said he. "Lift your heads. Look, a single cloud is drifting in the sky. It's very high and is slowly thinning out. In a few moments, it will be a mere thread dissolved in the blue. Look. You see, it no longer exists. All is blue. It's strange. There's no breeze today. The far-off mountain seems to be dreaming. Even the flies have stopped buzzing. All about us the orange trees are breathing in and out in silence. Why such calm, why such beauty?"

Amed and Aziz were silent.

"Halim. You know him? You don't want to answer? I know that you're acquainted with Halim. The other night, when Soulayed went silent, Halim's father, Kamal, spoke to me. His voice was not as strong as that of Soulayed. He said to me: 'Zahed, you have before you a great sinner. I do not deserve to be in your company. As Soulayed said, you are the worthy son of your father, Mounir, whose renown for a long time reached beyond the walls of his house. One must be in harmony with God to achieve what your father did with his two hands. How sad to look on his ruined house. How shameful. With what pain. Accept the poor prayers of the sinner I am. I strike my breast. I pray for the souls of your parents.'"

And Kamal, with his fist, had delivered three hard blows to his heart. Like this, Zahed asserted, reenacting in front of his sons Kamal's gesture.

"Kamal also said to me: 'God has blessed you twice, Zahed. Rejoice, that he has placed in your wife's womb two such sons. My wife died giving birth to our only son. Halim is what God has given me that is most precious. Yet I struck him. Look, you can still see the marks on his face. I struck him when he told me what he had decided. I closed my eyes and I struck him as I would strike a wall. I closed my eyes because I could not have struck my son in the light of day. When I opened my eyes, I saw blood. I closed my eyes and I struck harder. I opened my eyes. Halim had not moved. He stood tall before me and his eyes were filled with red tears. May God forgive me. I am only a miserable sinner. I did not understand. I did not want to understand his decision.'"

"'Now you understand your son's decision,' said Soulayed to Kamal before going to get the belt in his jeep.

"During Soulayed's absence, Halim leaned toward me and spoke as if he were revealing a secret.

"'Zahed, listen. Before my meeting with Soulayed, I cursed my mother. I cursed her because I did not die along with her. Why be born in a land that still seeks its name? I did not know my mother and I will never know my country. But Soulayed came to me. One day, he talked to me. He said: 'I know your father, I go to his shop to have my boots resoled. Kamal is a good worker. He asks a fair price for his labor. But he's an unhappy man. And you, his son, you are even more unhappy. Halim, to utter the word of God is not enough. I've watched you during prayers. Where is your strength? Why come to prostrate yourself among your brothers and beseech God's name? Your mouth is as empty as your heart. Who wants your unhappiness, Halim? Who can profit from your lament? You're already fifteen years old and you've done nothing with this life that God has offered you. In my eyes, you are worth no more than our enemies. Your softness weakens us and brings us shame. Where is your anger? I do not hear it. Listen to me, Halim: our enemies are dogs. They are like us, you think, because their faces are faces of men. That's an illusion. Look at them with the eyes of your ancestors, and you'll see what these faces are really made of. They are made of our death. In a single enemy face, you can see our annihilation a thousand times. Never forget this: every drop of your blood is a thousand times more precious than a thousand of their faces."

"When Soulayed came back with the belt, silence had taken hold of the night," said Zahed finally.

His two sons sat listening to him in the diaphanous shadow of the orange trees. Impressed by their father's story, Amed and Aziz understood that life in the orange grove would never be the same again. It was the second time in just a few short days that Zahed had spoken to them so seriously, he who was sparing with his words. He rose painfully and lit a cigarette. He smoked slowly, and with each puff seemed to be turning over in his head thoughts that were weighty, tormented.

"Halim is going to die," Zahed declared suddenly, butting out his cigarette. "At noon, when the sun is shining and at its zenith, Halim is going to die."

Zahed sat down near the boys, and all three waited in silence for the sun to locate itself right over their heads. At noon, Zahed asked his sons to look at the sun. They did so. First their eyes screwed up. Then they were able to keep them open. They filled with tears. Their father stared into the sun longer than they did.

"Halim is near to the sun now."

"Why?" asked Aziz.

"Dogs wearing clothes. Our enemies are dogs with clothes. They surround us. In the south, they have closed off our cities with walls of stone. That's where Halim has gone. He crossed the frontier. Soulayed told him how. He passed through a secret tunnel. Then he climbed onto a crowded bus. At noon, he blew himself up."

"But how?"

"With a belt of explosives, Aziz."

"Like the one we saw?"

"Yes, Amed, like the one you saw in the bag. Listen to me carefully: Soulayed, before he left, came to me and whispered something in my ear. He said to me: 'You have two sons. They were born at the foot of the mountain that closes off our land in the north. Few people know the secrets of this mountain as well as your two young sons. Have they not found a way to reach the other side? They've done it, no? You ask how I know that. Halim told me. And it's your sons themselves who told Halim.'"

Having said that, Zahed suddenly grabbed his sons by their necks. He held Amed with his right hand, and Aziz with his left. He lifted them from the ground. It was as if he'd gone mad. Amed and Aziz felt as if the earth had begun to shake, as if the oranges around them were going to fall by the thousands from their branches.

"Is that the truth?" cried their father. "What did you tell Halim? What did you tell that boy who just blew himself up?"

Unable to speak, Amed and Aziz began to cry.

That night, Zahed came to their room. They were already in bed. He leaned over them. In the shadows, his body was a shapeless mass. He talked very softly. Asked if they were sleeping. They didn't reply, but they weren't sleeping. Zahed continued to whisper.

"My little men," he said, "God knows what is in my heart. And you know too. You've always done me honor. You are brave sons. When the bomb fell on your grandparents' house, you showed great courage. Your mother is very proud of you. But she doesn't want to understand what is happening in our land. She doesn't want to see the danger facing us. She's very unhappy. She did not speak to Soulayed when he left. He's an important man. She insulted him. She shouldn't have done that. Soulayed will come back, you understand, he'll come back to talk to you. Now sleep."

He planted a kiss on Amed's brow. Then on that of Aziz, as he had done at the hospital. When he left, the smell of him lingered in the room.

Zahed was right. Soulayed came back very soon. Amed instantly recognized the sound of the jeep. He ran out of the house. Soulayed gestured for him to approach. This time Soulayed was alone. He asked Amed:

"Are you Amed or Aziz?"

"I'm Amed."

"Well, Amed, go and find your brother. I want to talk to both of you." Amed went into the house. Aziz was not yet up. Because he'd been sick, his mother was letting him sleep. Amed shook him: "Hurry up, get dressed. Soulayed's come. He wants to talk to us."

Aziz opened his eyes wide, raised his eyebrows in surprise. He looked like a little dog.

"Did you hear what I said? Get going! I'll wait for you downstairs."

"I'm coming," his brother mumbled, still half-asleep. A few minutes later, Amed and Aziz approached the jeep, both excited and suspicious.

"What are you waiting for, get in," Soulayed said to them, a smile on his lips. "Don't be afraid, I'm not going to eat you."

He shifted his machine gun into the backseat to make room for them beside him. When the jeep started up, Amed glimpsed his father in the orange grove. He moved toward the road and watched the jeep disappear into the distance.

Soulayed drove fast. The boys liked that. Aziz sat between Soulayed and his brother. No one talked. They left the road to take the dirt track leading to the mountain. The wind whistled. Blowing dust made their eyes burn. The boys saw the dead body of an animal. Soulayed avoided it with a jerk of the steering wheel. Amed asked what it was. Soulayed shrugged. A few minutes later, the jeep braked to a brutal halt. They could go no farther. The mountain rose up before them, blocking the horizon with its bluish mass. Soulayed got out of the jeep. Took a few steps.

"What's he doing?" Amed asked his brother in a low voice.

Suddenly they heard the sound of water. Stifling his laughter, Aziz said, "He's emptying his bladder."

After what was to them a long wait, Soulayed came back and sat in the jeep. Lit a cigarette. Took a deep drag and pointed to the mountain, there in front of them.

"A long time ago, I used to come here," he told them. "I was your age. A few friends and I rode around on our bikes. I would leave them by the side of the road and venture out on foot among the rocks. At that time, there were still wolves. But the wolves have disappeared. Now there are only snakes. There were woods, too, with giant cedars. Magnificent trees. Today only a handful are left in these parts. Look down there, maybe you'll see one. See it, where the land drops down? Well, this cedar, I know it like a brother. It's at least two thousand years old, and my biggest thrill when I was a child was to grab onto its branches and climb to the highest one! I was the only one among my friends who could do this. I wasn't afraid, even when I became dizzy. Once I had a good grip on the top branch, I spent hours just scanning the plain. Up there, I felt like another person. I saw the past and the future at the same time. I felt immortal . . . untouchable! I could look down on the two slopes of the mountain just by turning my head. On days when the sky was blue, my gaze soared like the outstretched wings of an eagle. Nothing could stand in its way. To the east, I saw the yellow earth of your grandfather. I thought he was mad. Planting trees on this side of the mountain! I shouted insults at him. I wasn't afraid. I knew very well that he couldn't hear me. No one could hear me when I was perched on top of this tree, no one!"

Soulayed stopped talking and scanned the sky as if he'd just heard an airplane. There was nothing in the sky, not even a bird. Soulayed took one last drag of his cigarette. He flicked the butt into the air, then grabbed his machine gun. He stood in the jeep and discharged his weapon in the direction of the cedar. The noise of the machine gun's burst took the boys' breath away. They huddled on the floor of the jeep. Soulayed threw down his weapon and grabbed them by their necks as their father had done in the orange grove. Soulayed had muscular arms. His whole person radiated strength.

"Guess," he said in a voice brimming with pride, "what I could see with my child's eyes when I turned to the west? Not this strip of arid land where your grandfather broke his fingers, no! To the west there was a valley where our ancestors had planted magnificent gardens. It was paradise. A pure miracle, I tell you! You could see in the distance, behind a long row of eucalyptus, the outskirts of a village. Between the houses, people had planted date and palm trees. Our land spread out all the way to the foot-hills leading to the immense chain of mountains bordering the ocean. On my perch, I recited at the top of my lungs the words of our great poet, Nahal:

Paradise is made of water, earth, sky,
and a gaze that nothing can obstruct.
The gaze is the secret element in space.
Never let it die.

"But if you were to climb to the top of this sick cedar today, what would you see?"

Soulayed shook one of the boys by the shoulders.

"Have you no answer? What would you see today?"

He shook Amed until it hurt. Still, Amed said nothing.

"Have you lost your tongue? Well?"

Amed was terrified. Soulayed got out of the jeep. Took a few steps. Then came back toward the boys. Kicked hard at one of the jeep's wheels. A bit of foam glistened at the edge of his lips.

"Your grandfather was right in the end," he cried bitterly. "He planted his oranges on the right side of the mountain! Go, get out of the jeep! Don't look at me like that. You know perfectly well why I brought you here."

Soulayed pushed the boys out of the jeep. Amed took his brother's hand. His own was shaking.

"You know this place. Before the bombings, you used to come here. I even saw you one day on your bicycles. You were coming here, no? I'm sure of it. And I know why. You told Halim. And Halim told me."

"We didn't tell Halim anything, he was lying," Amed replied in a hurry.

Soulayed smiled. He placed his hands on Amed's shoulders.

"Don't be afraid, child, you did nothing wrong."

Amed freed himself. Began to run toward the dirt road. Soulayed turned to the other boy. Asked him if he was Amed or Aziz.

"I'm Aziz."

Then he turned to Amed, who was running away. He cried to him: "Amed, Amed, listen to me, Halim told me about the day your kite string broke. I know what happened that day. God is great. He's the one who broke your string. Believe what I say, Amed! He broke it so that things would come to pass as they must."

Amed stopped running. Soulayed took Aziz's hand and led him toward his brother. All three sat down in the shadow of a rock.

"You came here to fly your kite. All the children around here know this is the best place for it. Since the bombings, no one risks coming here anymore, but you two came in spite of the danger. And your string broke and the kite, freed, flew off as if it wanted to rejoin, beyond the hills, the sea's immensity. Suddenly the wind stopped. As if by magic. You saw the kite fall from the sky and vanish on the other side of the mountain. And you went off to find it as if it were the most precious thing in the world. Paper and wind! I think it must have been fabulous, your kite. Full of bright colors. Maybe it was shaped like a bird or a dragon. Or maybe a dragonfly?"

"No, no, nothing like that," said Aziz. "It was our grandfather who'd made it. Just paper and wind, as you say."

"And you began to climb the mountain. Am I right? Answer me!"

"We had to go home with the kite, or our father would have had questions," Amed explained.

"Yes," Aziz went on. He began to imitate his father's voice: "Where did you lose it? You have no heart. Lose your grandfather's gift? Where did you go?"

"He would have waited for our answer," Amed

continued. "And we would have told the truth, we couldn't lie to our father."

"That's good, you must never lie to he who gave you life."

"Our father would have killed us," Aziz said, "if he'd learned that we came here. We had to go back with the kite. We began to climb the mountain. It wasn't very high. And there was the ghost of a road snaking through the rocks. It was easy to follow. We laughed. It was exciting to climb so high and to see the valley below and, very far off, the green spot of the orange grove."

"He who has the courage to rise up embraces his whole life at a glance. And also all his death."

Saying that, Soulayed smiled. He offered the boys cigarettes. They smoked, sitting all three on the ground that became, despite the shade, more and more scorching. Soulayed's neck shone with sweat.

"Your grandfather was right in the end. In his day he planted orange trees on the good side of the mountain. Because on the other side, our dead were being ripped out of their tombs. The living were massacred, their houses destroyed.

Their fields and their gardens were razed. Each day that passes, our enemies gnaw away at the land of our ancestors. They are rats!"

Soulayed took a long drag on his cigarette.

"Well, Amed, and you, Aziz, when you reached the top, what did you see on the other side?"

"The other side of the sky," replied Aziz. "I saw the other side of the sky. There was no end. As if my eyes couldn't reach any farther. And then, in the dust blown up by the wind, I saw in the distance a town, a strange kind of town."

"It wasn't a town," Amed corrected. "It didn't look like a town. At each end there was a tower that threw flashes of light into the sky."

"Military installations, that's what you saw. You saw warehouses surrounded by barbed wire. And do you know what's inside? Our death. They've been planning it for years. But God broke your kite string and now it's their own death they're warehousing."

Amed and Aziz didn't understand Soulayed's last words. They wondered if he was losing his mind.

"You knew you'd go to the other side of the

mountain. Who doesn't? We've been at war for so long. You knew it, no? And that's what you told Halim."

"No! We didn't know it!"

"Don't lie!"

"My brother doesn't lie!" shouted Aziz, standing up. "He only told Halim that our kite flew over the mountain."

"I just wanted to impress him, that's all," added Amed, tears in his voice. "Halim was the best kite flyer around. I didn't do anything wrong."

"Listen to me, both of you. It doesn't matter what you knew or didn't know. And it doesn't matter what you really told Halim. Those are childish things and we don't need to talk about them anymore. Do you want to know what really happened that day?"

Soulayed stood up without waiting for their answer, and set off with long strides toward the mountain.

"Follow me!"

They walked under the sun for a good ten minutes before they came to the foot of the mountain.

"Around here, I imagine, was where you climbed the mountain to find your kite?"

"Yes," Aziz admitted.

"Right there," his brother added.

"Just what I thought."

Soulayed wrapped his arms around the two boys.

"You didn't know that with every step you took, you could have been blown up by a mine. You didn't know that, did you?"

Soulayed stroked the boys' heads.

"A miracle is what really happened that day. God broke your kite string and God guided your steps on the mountain."

They returned to the road in silence. Aziz felt like throwing up because of the cigarette Soulayed had given him.

Back at the jeep, Soulayed burst out laughing. He picked up a bottle of water lying at his feet. It was half-full. He opened it and poured its contents over his head. The water washed over his hair and his beard and wet his shirt. His laughter frightened the boys. He turned to them with a big grin. His white teeth were beautiful, perfect. He started the motor. Amed didn't dare say that he was thirsty too. He searched with his eyes to see if another bottle was lying around. There was no other. Soulayed drove faster than he had on the way there. He said in a loud voice, speaking over the noise of the jeep and the wind: "Do you see now what you've accomplished? You found a road to lead you to that strange town. You're the only ones who've done it. Others who've tried to do so were blown to smithereens by the mines. In a few days, one of you will go back there. You, Aziz, or you, Amed. Your father will decide. And the one who is chosen will wear a belt of explosives. He will go down to that strange town and make it disappear forever."

Before leaving them, Soulayed said again: "God has chosen you. God has blessed you."

Amed took refuge in the house. For a long time, Aziz stood watching the cloud of dust stirred up by the jeep's departure.

While the boys waited for Soulayed to return, time became strangely long. Minutes stretched out as if made of dough. One of the brothers would be going off to war to blow up military installations in the strange town, as Soulayed had called it. They talked about it all the time. Who would their father choose? Why one rather than the other? Aziz swore that he wouldn't let his brother go off without him. Amed said the same thing. Despite their youth, they were aware of the honor Soulayed was conferring on them. Suddenly they had become real fighters.

To kill time, they played at blowing themselves up in the orange grove. Aziz had stolen an old belt from his father that they weighted with three tin cans full of sand. They took turns wearing it, slipping into the skin of a future martyr. The orange trees also played war with them. The trees became enemies, endless rows of warriors poised to launch their explosive fruits at the slightest suspicious noise. The boys worked their way between them, crawling and scraping their knees. When they activated the detonator—an old shoelace—trees were uprooted by the force of the explosion, shooting into the sky in a thousand fragments, falling back down onto their shredded bodies.

Amed and Aziz tried to imagine the impact of that fatal moment.

"Do you think it will hurt?"

"No, Amed."

"Are you sure? And Halim?"

"What about Halim?"

"There must be little pieces of Halim all over now."

"I guess so."

"Do you think that's a problem?"

"Why a problem?"

"For going to heaven."

"Think, Amed. It doesn't matter what happens on earth. The real Halim, the whole Halim, is already in heaven."

"That's what I think too, Aziz."

"Then what are you worried about?"

"Nothing. Yesterday I had a dream. Our father had chosen me. Before leaving, I gave you my yellow truck."

"What yellow truck?"

"The one in my dream."

"You never had a yellow truck."

"In my dream I had one. I gave it to you. And I left with the belt."

"And me?"

"What?"

"What did I do when you left with the belt?"

"You played with the yellow truck."

"That's a stupid dream, Amed."

"You're the one who's stupid!"

The two brothers looked at each other in silence for a long moment. Each tried to guess what the other was thinking. Aziz saw tears well up in his brother's gaze.

"Aziz, do you sometimes hear voices?"

"What do you mean?"

"Voices in your head."

"No, Amed."

"Never?"

"Never."

Amed was disappointed by his brother's answer.

In the beginning, he'd thought everyone heard voices. "If that's how it is . . ." But in time, Amed had come to the conclusion that he might be the only person in the universe to have had such an experience. No one around him had mentioned any such thing. Only that once had he found the courage to talk about it to his grandmother, but it was impossible to describe the strange words that came without warning.

The voices reeled off incoherent sounds inside him, turned words inside out, end-lessly repeated a sentence he'd just said or that his brother or his mother had spoken the day before. Amed felt as if he harbored within him-self a tiny Amed, a kernel of himself made of material much harder than his own flesh, and that had several mouths, like his character Dôdi. Sometimes the voices spoke as if they knew more than Amed himself did. Perhaps they'd been born before him? Perhaps they'd lived elsewhere before settling inside him? Per-haps, when he slept, they traveled and absorbed knowledge inaccessible to him? Perhaps they knew languages other than his own. Despite the times when they deformed words or babbled them senselessly, perhaps these voices had important things to tell him?

Zahed spent several days cleaning up the debris of his parents' house. He cleared the property around it as well. Salvaged photos, clothes, some dishes. But he didn't keep the few sticks of furniture that were still usable. Tamara helped him as much as she could. The boys offered to lend a hand, but their father chased them away. Husband and wife worked in silence. Silence that was heavy and painful. Several times, Tamara wanted to open her mouth and as many times she held back. It was the same for Zahed. A truck came to collect what was left of the house's walls. There was nothing now but the floor stained with blood. Zahed took his wife by the hand. She didn't understand what he wanted to do. Seeing her unease, he asked her to sit down. She obeyed. He sat near her on the floor bereft of walls, mourning those who had lived there. Tamara wanted to laugh. She felt like her in-laws' house had been swept away by the wind, and that she and her husband were on the verge of uprooting themselves from the earth in turn, leaving it for good.

Zahed broke the silence: "It will be Amed. He's the one who will wear the belt." Tamara's heart stopped.

"I know what you're thinking," Zahed went on, painfully. "I know what you want to say. I've thought about this for a long time. It won't be Aziz. I'd be ashamed, Tamara. I couldn't go on living if I asked Aziz to wear the belt. I couldn't face God. Yes, Tamara, I've thought about it for a long time. I've turned the question over thousands of times in my heart, and . . ."

"But Aziz will . . ." Tamara couldn't finish her sentence.

"Yes, Aziz will die, I know it as well as you do. I told you what the doctor explained to me. It would not be a sacrifice if he wore the belt. It would be an offense. And it would be turned against us. Also, Aziz could not succeed in his present state. He's too weak. No, Tamara, it can't be Aziz. You don't send a sick child to war. You don't sacrifice what has already been sacrificed. Try to think it through, Tamara, you'll come to the same conclusion. It's Amed who will go."

Tamara wept and shook her head no, unable to speak.

"Why do you think Soulayed came to offer me his condolences and brought Kamal with him? Listen to me, this man lost his wife when his only son was born. And he agreed to sacrifice him."

Zahed rose. Tamara watched him move off, his back bent, into the orange grove. She was not surprised. She had known Zahed would choose Amed. In her heart, she had always known. And it rendered her mute with pain.

That night, in the garden, she looked at the moon, bathed herself in its distant light. Suddenly she remembered a song. Her mother had murmured it into her ear to put her to sleep:

One day we will be light.
We will live with eyes always open.
But tonight, child, close your eyelids.

A sensation of cold seized hold of her belly. She thought she was going to be sick. But the cold, which usually moved downwards, now climbed as high as her lips, her tongue. Icy words formed in her mouth. She realized it was too late. Nothing could melt those words and the thoughts they contained. She waited for night to envelop the house, then she went up, silently, to the boys' room. She heard the whistling of their breath. They were sleeping deeply. She approached Amed's bed, and placed her hand on his brow. She waited for him to wake. When his eyes were half-open, she tenderly took his hand.

"Don't say anything, don't wake your brother, follow me."

They slipped out of the bedroom like thieves. With Amed, she went back into the garden. They sat down on the "moon bench," as Tamara secretly liked to call it. Amed didn't seemed too surprised that she'd woken him in the middle of the night and led him out of the house. His eyelids were still heavy with sleep.

"Listen to me, Amed. Soon your father will go into your room without a sound, so as not to wake your brother, and will place his hand on your head as I did myself just now. And you, you'll slowly emerge from your sleep and you'll understand, seeing his face bent over yours, that it's you he's chosen. Or he'll take you by the hand, lead you into the orange grove, and sit you down at the foot of a tree to talk to you. I don't know just how your father will reveal it to you, but you'll know before he's even opened his mouth. Do you realize what that means? You will not come back from the mountain. I don't know what all Soulayed has told you, you and your brother, but I can guess. Your father says he's a man who can see the future. An important man who is shielding us from our enemies. Everyone respects him, no one dares disobey him. Your father fears him. Me, as soon as I saw him, I found him arrogant. Your father should not have allowed him to cross the threshold of our house. Who has given him the right to go into people's houses and take away their children? I'm not stupid. I know that we're in a war and that we must make sacrifices. And I know that you and your brother are coura- geous. You've told your father that it would be an honor for you to fulfill your duty and wear this belt. He told me what you said. You're ready to follow in the steps of Halim and all the others. Your father is overwhelmed. He's proud of your determination. God has given us the two best sons in the world, but Amed, I am not the best mother in the world. You remember my cousin Hajmi? You remember, don't you? She was sick. Aziz suffers from the same sickness. His bones are decaying, melting away inside his body. Your brother is going to die, Amed."

"I don't believe it."

"Don't tell your mother she's lying. The big-city doctor told your father. Aziz will not see the next harvest. Don't cry, my dear, it's too hard, I beg you, don't cry."

"Mama."

"Listen to me, Amed, listen to me. I don't want you to wear the belt."

"What are you saying?"

"I don't want to lose both my sons. Talk to your brother, persuade him to take your place."

"Never."

"Tell him you don't want to wear the belt."

"It's not true."

"Tell him you're afraid."

"No!"

"Oh, Amed, my child. Aziz will be happier if he dies over there! You know what's ahead of him otherwise? He'll die in his bed, suffering horribly. Don't deprive him of a glorious death for which God will welcome him with all the honors due a martyr. I beg you, ask Aziz to take your place. Don't tell anyone, above all not your father. It will be our secret unto death."

Amed headed back to bed like a tottering little ghost. Tamara remained sitting on the moon bench. She struggled to calm her heart. After a long time, she held out her hand to the nearest rose. She stroked its petals with her fingertips. Tamara thought she could see the flower's heart breathing in and out. "The scent of flowers is their blood," Shahina had said to her one day. "Flowers are generous and brave. They shed their blood without caring for their lives. That's why they fade so fast, worn out from offering their beauty to whoever wants to lay eyes on it." Shahina had planted this rosebush when the twins were born. It was her way of celebrating the arrival of her grandsons. Tamara quickly got up from the bench and brusquely tore off the roses. Her hands bled, scratched by the thorns. She felt horrible. That terrible thought, she'd given it voice: she'd sent her sick son to his death.

The next day, a voice woke Amed well before his brother. To his amazement, it possessed the accents and unique rhythms of Halim's voice. No mistake, it was really his. It spoke inside Amed without really speaking to him, as if it were a song sung by someone who didn't need to be listened to in order to exist.

"My string has broken . . . my string has broken . . ." repeated Halim's voice.

For a moment, Amed thought the young man with the belt was in his room, back from the land of the dead.

"My string broke . . . it's not the wind's fault . . . an awful noise has broken my string . . . my ears are bleeding . . . I can't hear anything any more . . ."

Amed sat up in bed and looked around. He saw no one in the half light of the room. There was no one but his brother sleeping beside him.

"I come close to the sun . . . I climb . . . I climb . . . it's not the wind's fault . . . it's because of the noise . . . I don't hear anything anymore and I can't see the earth anymore . . . the white clouds swallow me up . . . no one can see me anymore . . ."

Amed held his hands over his ears, but the voice only got stronger.

"A cruel noise has broken my string . . . I'm burning . . . alone in this huge sky . . . I'll return no more . . . I'm burning . . . alone in the absence of the wind . . ."

Amed got up and went to his bedroom window. Dawn. The sun's first rays were touching the tops of the orange trees. For a long time he watched the sky turn blue. The voice calmed down bit by bit. When it had gone totally silent, he went back to bed. He heard his heart beating. He hugged Aziz tightly. He pressed his body against his brother's, as if to merge with him.

Had he dreamed it, or had his mother really said that his brother's bones were melting? Had he dreamed it, or had his mother really said that it would be better for his brother if his bones exploded on the other side of the mountain? The body he was embracing suddenly

seemed so brittle . . . no, he would not let Aziz
wear the belt in his place.

Aziz woke and pushed him away abruptly.

"What are you doing, Amed?"

"Nothing. Get up, it's late."

The cruel death of his parents had not changed Zahed's routine. On the contrary, he worked with even more determination. In his eyes, the orange grove had increased in value. It was now the sanctuary where the bodies of his parents lay. He went over every tree, removed rotten branches, irrigated the soil, all with the sense of performing sacred gestures. The perfume that rose from the earth comforted him, helped him believe that the future still had meaning. He felt safe among his trees, as if no bomb could breach the armor of their greenery. His heart knew it: these fields of oranges were his only friends.

Leaning back against a tree, Zahed had nevertheless let his tears flow that day. He thought of his father. What would he have done? Would he have chosen Amed or Aziz? Sitting beneath the foliage of an orange tree he had just pruned, he waited for a sign from his dead father. All morning Zahed pondered what he would say to Amed.

"In any case," he said to himself at last, "there's no point in sending one to his death, knowing death has already touched the other one with his invisible hand. But what else to do?"

He dried his tears and left the orange grove. Near the house, he saw his sons playing in the garden. They had just left their mother and her improvised class in the kitchen. Hesitant, he approached them. Amed and Aziz felt his presence and went to meet him, astonished that their father was not working at this hour. Zahed looked on his two sons in silence, as if he were seeing them for the first time, or the last. He didn't quite know what to call the emotions that were constricting his throat. He took Amed by the hand and led him away, leaving Aziz confused.

"Where are you taking me?"

But Amed knew what his father had in mind. Zahed maintained his silence, gripping his son's hand more tightly. They walked to the toolshed. His father gave him a key and asked him to open the big iron padlock. Amed obeyed. Then Zahed pushed open the heavy wooden door. When they went into the shed, two birds escaped through an open skylight above their heads. For a moment Amed was afraid. The door closed behind them. A ray of sun shone down from the roof, millions of dust motes dancing in the long blade of light. It smelled of oil and wet earth. "This is where I've stored it," murmured Zahed. He went into a corner and lifted up an old tarpaulin. He came back to his son with the canvas bag Soulayed had brought. He crouched down and had Amed sit near him.

"You have to shut the dead into the ground," he said, as if every word he articulated was itself rising from the earth's depths. "Because that's how . . . that's how the dead enter heaven. By being shut into the ground. That's how I buried my parents. You saw me, I took my old shovel and I dug a hole. You saw the worms arriving to celebrate the burial. The hardest thing wasn't throwing earth into the hole to cover it up. You saw me, I covered the hole completely. The hardest part was searching through the debris. My mother, I saw her head cracked open. I could no longer see the goodness of her face. Blood, there was blood on the broken walls, on the shattered plates. With my bare hands I scooped up what was left of my father. There was no end. I asked you, your brother and yourself, not to come near. I asked it also of your mother. No one ought to have to do that. No one, not even the guiltiest of men, ought to have to recover what's left of their parents in the ruins of their house. I dug the hole that splits the sky in two, as our ancestors said. And I heard the deadly boring buzz of flies, as our ancestors also said. My son, one must not fear death."

From sentence to sentence, Zahed's voice softened in the semidarkness of the shed. Amed found it unsettling and at the same time comforting to hear his father talking to him this way.

"We live every day in the fear that it will be our last. We don't sleep very well and when we do sleep, nightmares stalk us. Entire villages are destroyed every week. Our dead grow in number. The war gets worse, Amed. We have no choice. The bomb that destroyed your grandparents' house came from the other side of the mountain. You know that, right? More bombs will come from that cursed place. Every morning, when I open my eyes and see that the orange grove is still there under the sun, I thank God for this miracle. Amed, if I could, I would take your place. Your mother, too, wouldn't hesitate for a second. Nor your brother. Especially your brother, who loves you so much. Soulayed will return. It's he who will take you to the foot of the mountain. He'll come back soon with his jeep, in a few days or perhaps in a few weeks, but certainly before the harvest. It's you who will wear the belt."

Zahed opened the canvas bag. His hands trembled slightly. Amed saw this despite the shed's dim light. Watching his father, Amed imagined that he was extricating something from the bag that was alive, grey or green, a mysterious and dangerous animal.

"I must tell you something else. Your brother is not yet cured. He could not wear the belt. He's too weak. That's why I chose you."

"And if Aziz were not sick, who would you have chosen?" asked Amed, with a composure that surprised his father.

For a long moment, Zahed didn't know how

to answer his son, who was already regretting the question. Amed knew that his brother was very sick, and that he would never be cured. Tamara had left no doubt in Amed's mind as to the seriousness of Aziz's illness. He was going to die. Just like Amed, if he didn't trade places with his brother.

"I would have asked the oranges to decide in my stead."

"The oranges?"

"Here's what I would have done: I'd have given an orange to your brother, and another to you. The one who found the most seeds in his orange, he's the one who would have left."

Amed smiled. Zahed stood up. The way he held the belt of explosives in his hands lent the object a solemn importance. Amed then saw that it was not at all like what he and his brother had cobbled together to amuse themselves. It seemed heavy and malign. Amed went near and touched it gingerly.

"Do you want to take it?"

"Isn't it dangerous?" asked Amed, drawing back a step.

"No. It's not connected to the detonator. You

know, that's what will enable you to . . . well, you know what I mean."

Amed knew what a detonator was. His father handed him the belt.

"Soulayed made me understand that you should love the belt. That you should see it as part of yourself. You can wear it whenever you like. You must accustom yourself to its weight, to its touch. But never take it out of here. You understand? And above all, don't come here with your brother. That would only complicate things."

"I promise."

"You're not afraid?"

"No," Amed lied, "I'm not afraid."

"You're brave. I'm proud of you. We're all proud of you."

There was a long silence, during which Zahed no longer dared to look at his son.

"Here, this is the key to the lock. From now on, you can come here whenever you want."

Zahed bent over Amed and placed a kiss on his brow. Then he walked away. When he opened the door, light streamed into the shed, blinding Amed. Once the door was closed, he found himself again in darkness, the belt in his hands. He hardly dared breathe. Suddenly, he thought he saw a face appear, floating in space.

"Grandfather, is it you?"

Amed was certain he'd seen his grandfather Mounir's face. He knew he was dead and buried in the orange grove, but the vision was so powerful that he called out again.

"Answer me, grandfather, is it you?"

As his eyes became accustomed to the darkness, Amed again made out the shed's walls, and the tools lined up on makeshift shelves. The sun from the skylight made the scythes glimmer, along with the pruning shears and the ends of the shovels and saws. Amed glanced around him. The vision had vanished for good. He breathed deeply and placed the belt around his waist. His muscles tensed. He took a few hesitant steps.

"Now I'm a real soldier."

Crouched behind a bush in the garden, Aziz saw his father leave the shed without Amed and go back to work in the orange grove. He wasn't surprised at his father's choice. He waited for Amed to follow him out, but in vain. After a long while, Aziz decided to go and join Amed in the shed. Slowly, he opened the big door a crack.

"Amed, what are you doing?"

His brother didn't reply, so he stepped inside.

"I know you're there. Answer me."

"Don't come in."

"Why?"

"Leave me alone."

Aziz advanced, slowly making out his brother's silhouette in the half light.

"What are you doing?"

"Don't come near me."

"Why?"

"It's dangerous."

Aziz froze. He heard his brother breathing noisily.

"What's the matter?"

"I can't move."

"Are you sick?"

"Leave."

"Why?"

"I'm wearing the belt and if I move . . ."

"You're ridiculous!"

"Everything will blow up. Go away!"

"I'm going to get Father," said Aziz, frightened.

"You believed me? You're stupid," Amed shouted with a laugh, running at his brother so fast that he knocked him to the ground. "You're really stupid. The belt has no detonator!"

Aziz grabbed his brother's legs, and threw him to the ground in turn. The two fought wildly.

"I'll kill you!"

"Give me the belt, I'm the one who should go!"

"I'm the one Father chose, I'm the one who has to go."

"I want to try it, take it off!"

"Never!"

Aziz hit his brother in the face. Amed stood up, dizzied. He took hold of a long scythe leaning against a wall.

"Come near and I'll carve you into little pieces."

"Try!"

"I'm serious, Aziz."

The two brothers eyed each other without moving, each listening to the other's shallow breathing. They were still merely children. Something had changed, as if the darkness had imposed on their young bodies a density and a gravitas only an adult body could bear.

"I'm afraid to die, Aziz."

Amed put down the scythe. His brother went to him.

"I know. I'll go."

"You can't."

"I will go, Amed."

"We can't disobey Father."

"I'll take your place. Father won't know."

"He'll notice."

"No. Believe me. Take it off," begged Aziz.

Amed hesitated, then removed the belt with an abrupt gesture. Aziz took it and went to the back of the shed, to where the sunbeam from the skylight almost touched the ground. In the dancing light he scrutinized the object that would slaughter his people's enemies and usher him into paradise. He was fascinated. The belt was made up of a dozen small cylindrical compartments filled with explosives.

Amed came to join him. "Do you think the dead can come back?"

"I don't know."

"I think I saw Grandfather a while ago."

"Where?"

"There," said Amed, pointing to a spot in front of them.

"Are you sure?"

"It was his face. He disappeared right away."

"You saw a ghost."

"When you die, maybe you'll come back too."

"Let's get out of here," Aziz said anxiously.

Amed put the belt back in the canvas bag he'd hidden under the old tarp. When the two brothers emerged from the shed, the light of day hurt their eyes.

Amed went to join his mother, who was in the kitchen preparing the evening meal, chopping vegetables on a wooden board. She poured rice onto the page of an old newspaper, and asked her son to pick it over. Amed liked helping his mother cook, even if he was a bit ashamed of it. It was unusual for a boy. When he'd first begun offering to help her, Tamara, looking surprised, had refused. He'd asked again, and in the end she'd accepted. Since then, she had cherished and sought out these moments with her son. When Amed went several days without making a little visit to the kitchen, she worried and wondered whether Zahed had spoken to him. She knew that her husband found such behavior inappropriate for a boy.

Amed was concentrating on his task, picking

little stones and pieces of dirt out of the rice. His moves were rapid and precise. Tamara dared not ask the question that was burning her lips. She waited for her son to break the unusual silence that was growing between them. These moments they shared were generally an opportunity for conversations they couldn't otherwise have. The feeling of complicity between mother and son sometimes had them laughing out loud. Amed also took these opportunities to talk about his aunt Dalimah, whom he missed. Every one of the letters he received from his aunt was special to him. At first, his mother had read them to him. But since he'd learned to make out words, he would reread his aunt's letters for hours. She told stories about her new life. She described the subway, a train that passed through neighborhoods under the city's streets and buildings! She talked to him about the snow that, in just a few hours, covered the roofs of houses and brought a woolly silence down from the sky. The few photos she slipped into the envelopes astonished him and made him all the more curious. Amed especially liked the ones where you saw the city lit up at night, or those showing high bridges

and the river they spanned with their steel struc-
tures, and the blinking ribbon of automobile
headlights. She was careful never to send photos of her husband. His aunt once wrote that she
thought of the orange grove every time she ate
an orange. She would have loved to see it again,
to walk between the rows of trees with her little
Amed, breathing in along with him the perfume
surrounding their white flowers in the summer.

"It's done," Amed said suddenly to his mother.

Tamara thought he'd finished sorting the
rice. She looked at her son and understood,
relieved, that he was talking about the switch.

"Did you ask him?"

"Yes, today in the . . ."

"You didn't let on that he was sick?"

"No!"

"You mustn't."

"No! I did like you said."

"You said you were afraid, is that right?"

"Yes. I told him I was afraid of dying."

"My poor Amed! Forgive me! Forgive me!
I know you're brave, just like your brother. It's
horrible, what I'm asking of you, so horrible . . ."

"Don't cry, Mama."

"What's the use of bringing children into the world if it's just to sacrifice them like poor animals being sent to the slaughterhouse!"

"Don't cry anymore."

"No, I'm not crying anymore. You see, I've stopped crying. And we've done this for Aziz, you mustn't forget. Now finish sorting the rice."

Tamara dried her tears and lit a fire under the big pot.

"You have to be careful about one thing, Amed."

"What, Mama?"

"Your brother, since he's been sick, has grown thinner."

"Not really."

"But yes! Haven't you noticed? His cheeks are not as round as yours. He has less appetite than you do. Watch your brother's plate, and make sure you eat less than him. I feel terrible having to ask you that, so terrible, but swear to me that you'll do it, Amed!"

"Yes, I'll do it."

"Your father mustn't be aware of the switch. It would be horrible if he discovered it. I don't dare even think about it."

"Don't worry. In a few days, I'll be as thin as Aziz, and no one will be able to tell us apart."

"I will."

"Yes, you, but only you."

"I'd understand if you hated me."

"Here, I'll finish sorting the rice."

"Thank you, Amed."

"I'll never hate you."

"I'm going to cut myself with a knife."

"Why?"

"We'll do the switch at the last minute."

"What are you talking about, Aziz?"

"When you're about to leave with Soulayed, I'm going to arrange to wound myself with a knife. But not really. You, on the other hand, have to do it for real."

"I don't understand what you're saying."

"You only have to make a little cut. On your left hand. Don't make a mistake, Amed, it has to be the left hand."

"All right. But I still don't see why."

"I'm going to take blood from a sheep."

"Blood from a sheep!" repeated Amed, completely perplexed.

"To make them believe I've hurt myself. I'll

put it on my hand and wrap it in a cloth. When we switch, I'll wash it. No one will see the wound on my hand. But you, everyone will see yours."

"Because I'll really be cut," said Amed, beginning to grasp what his brother was up to.

"That's it. There will be no doubt. You'll be Aziz with the wounded hand, and I'll be Amed, ready to leave with Soulayed."

"Aziz with the wounded hand," repeated Amed with a sigh.

The two brothers were lying on the roof of the house. The first stars had just come out. They pierced the sky one by one, before riddling it by the dozen with sparkling points of light. Amed and Aziz had got in the habit of climbing up there to take advantage of the breeze. They lay on their backs near the big water tank, gazing far into the endless night.

"Don't be sad, Amed. Soon I'll be up there. Promise me you'll come here every night to tell me about your day."

"How will I be able to find you? There are so many stars."

"Come, let's go to bed. I'm cold."

Amed touched his brother's forehead. It was very hot.

"Are you sick?"

"Just tired. Come. Maybe Soulayed will be here tomorrow. Let's go to sleep."

Over the next days, Aziz behaved like a little general with his brother, giving him orders all the time. Amed let himself be guided, impressed by the boy who would soon be sacrificing his life.

Aziz kept saying that Amed shouldn't worry, that everything would go well. It was very simple. They had to learn to do everything the same way. Though they were identical twins, their parents rarely mistook them. Only their grandmother had confused them all the time, to the point where they'd suspected her of doing so on purpose in order to make fun of them. And so their resemblance had to be not only physical, but also expressed by their behavior.

"You see, you move like a frightened bird."

"Not at all," retorted Amed.

"Yes you do! You're nervous. You keep making little jumps instead of taking steps."

"And you! You walk like a sleeping fish."

"Idiot! Fish don't walk."

"No, but if they walked, they would walk like you!"

"Listen, I'm going to stop dragging my feet, and you're going to put yours firmly on the ground with every step. Then we'll be walking the same way. Let's try!"

Aziz continued giving his brother lessons so that all the differences between them would disappear. He pointed out to Amed the gestures he had to avoid making, and the few intonations that might imperil their switch. It became a game like any other, except in this game there would be no winner. Curiously, Aziz made no reference to their most obvious difference, which would almost certainly betray them if anyone took the time to look at the brothers side by side: Aziz's thinness. It was as if he were oblivious to the weight he had lost since he fell ill. As his mother had suggested, Amed made sure he didn't finish his meals, and even went so far as to sneak some of his own food onto his brother's plate. Tamara sometimes helped Amed by serving him less and giving Aziz a double portion. But she had to stop one day when Aziz asserted that she was being unjust to his brother. She was afraid he'd discover their collusion. Tamara cursed herself several times a day. She was ashamed and felt as guilty as if she had plotted with one of her sons to poison the other in small doses, whereas she loved them both with all her heart. But she was determined that this endless war would not rob her of both sons. And so when Amed was not losing weight fast enough, Tamara suggested he make himself vomit after the evening meal. After all, her husband had told her that Soulayed would be back before the approaching harvest. Amed pushed his finger down his throat and threw up his food, tears streaming down his cheeks.

They saw their parents leave for the village. Their father had borrowed the neighbor's truck. They were going to buy pesticides. Tamara had insisted on going along. She liked trips to the village: breaking her routine, meeting other women who were also doing errands. She brought back treats for the boys and occasionally, though they were hard to find, illustrated comic books.

Once the truck had disappeared along the road, Aziz grabbed his brother by the arm and pulled him toward the shed.

"Come on, let's not waste any time! You have the key?"

"I always have it on me."

Aziz was anxious to see the explosives belt again. Amed opened the lock while glancing at the road to be sure his father hadn't turned back.

Aziz rushed into the shed and pulled the canvas bag out from under the tarp.

"Let's go into the orange grove!"

"It's too dangerous."

"No it isn't. They won't be back for at least an hour. Come on, Amed, come!"

Amed followed his brother reluctantly. They sat down beneath the foliage of a big orange tree. Its perfume mellowed the air. Bees buzzed in the high branches. His breathing shallow, Aziz pulled the belt out of the bag.

"It's heavy."

"Father said you had to get used to its weight."

"Give me the key, I want to keep it with me. As soon as I can, I'll go into the shed to try on the belt. I have to be ready when I leave."

With misgivings, Amed gave his brother the key. Aziz stood up to try the belt, and took a few awkward steps.

"You have to hide it under your shirt."

"I know, I'm not crazy."

"So do it!"

"I'll decide when I want to do it."

"All right, don't get mad."

"I'm not mad."

"So why are you shouting, Aziz?"

Aziz went off, snaking through the trees. He paused, hid behind a tree trunk, watched for enemies, ran to another trunk. He ended his game by scrambling with some difficulty onto an enormous rock. Long ago his grandfather, after many fruitless attempts to dislodge it, had reconciled himself to its presence in the midst of his trees. "After all," he'd thought, "this rock might have come from heaven." Zahed had sworn to himself that he'd break it down with a sledgehammer, but he, too, had given up.

With a scream that made Amed jump, Aziz blew himself up, in the hope that the orange grove would be rid, once and for all, of that solitary and stubborn rock. His arms in the air, he imagined a rain of little fragments striking him on the head, forgetting for a moment that if he followed this thought to its conclusion, his body would also be part of the debris falling from the shaken sky.

"I did it!"

"What?"

"Don't you see? I blew it up."

"Blew what up?"

"The rock."

"I don't see anything."

"Imagine it, stupid!"

"I don't feel like imagining anything today."

"What's wrong, Amed?"

"Do you ever think about Aunt Dalimah?"

"What about her?"

"You never answer her letters."

"I don't want to talk about her. Do you know why?"

"Is it because of her husband?"

"He's one of those people who shoot bombs at us from the other side of the mountain."

"Maybe he's different."

"No. Father says they're all dogs. You heard him. And you heard Soulayed."

"We'd better go back into the shed now, don't you think?"

As the two brothers were shutting the heavy shed door behind them, they heard a motor.

"Father's back," murmured Amed.

"No, that doesn't sound like the neighbor's truck."

An instant later, a door slammed. Then they heard someone approaching.

"Come on, Aziz, let's hide in the back."

They had just enough time to slide under the tarp, near the tools, before the door cracked open with a slow creaking sound. A man entered, took a few steps, then stopped. The two boys held their breaths.

"I know you're there. I saw you from the road. Why are you hiding? Ah, I think I'm burning!"

The man leaned over the tarp.

"There are some really big rats here. Fortunately, there's an excellent shovel whiling away its time right there. All I have to do is to take it and slam it down on those nasty rats that think they're invisible," Soulayed joked. "Come on out, I have to talk to you. Go find your father."

"He's not here," said Aziz, poking his head out from under the tarp.

"He's gone to the village with our mother," added Amed quickly.

The boys came out of their hiding place. In the shadows, Soulayed could make out the uneasy brightness of their eyes.

"So is it you your father's chosen?"

Aziz nervously hid with his arms the explosives belt he'd not had time to take off.

"That belt you're wearing is not a toy."

"I know."

"Are you Amed or Aziz?"

"I'm . . . I'm Amed," Aziz lied.

"Amed. Well. Amed, be blessed."

Soulayed took from his jacket pocket a bundle of money neatly tied up with string.

"Here, give this to your father. It's a gift, compensation for what happened to your grandparents. Your father will need it. And your mother will be happy. You know, Amed, what's going to happen is both sad and happy. You understand, right? But you, you must just be happy. You're going to die a martyr. You are three times blessed."

Aziz took the money without saying a word. He'd never seen so much.

"Prepare yourself, Amed. I'll be back in two days."

Soulayed left them in a heavy silence. He opened the shed door with a sharp blow and disappeared in a burst of dust-churned light. Amed and Aziz waited for the noise of his jeep to die away before emerging from their lethargy. Aziz took off the belt and put it back in its hiding place.

"Here, Amed, take the money. It's you who'll be giving it to Father."

"You're right. Now let's get out of here."

Aziz locked the shed door and gave the key to his brother.

"You don't want to keep it?"

"Didn't you hear Soulayed? I'm going to leave in two days. I won't have any more chances to come back to the shed."

Aziz then looked at his brother with such intensity that Amed turned away and started to run for no reason, disappearing into the fields of orange trees.

Sadness reigned in the house. The air was heavy in spite of the breeze from the open windows. The house gave off a silence, as the orange trees gave off light. It was as if the walls, the floor, and the furniture all knew that Soulayed would be returning the next day.

All day Aziz whispered to his brother that he was happy, that all would go well.

Amed wanted to fold his brother in his arms and make Aziz disappear in his embrace, so that no one could take him away. Aziz was going to die like Halim. Amed would never see him again on earth. Aziz had promised that he would wait for Amed at the gates to Paradise. He would even wait if Amed grew as old as their uncle Bhoudir, who had died at the age of ninety-seven. And then they would be together again.

When night came, Zahed brought them all together in the house. He'd invited some neighbors and the two employees who helped him in the orange grove. With ardent pride, he explained that his young son Amed would soon be a martyr. All saw this invitation as an honor being bestowed on them.

Tamara had prepared a meal worthy of a great celebration. She'd hung from the ceiling a garland of bulbs that washed the room in multicolored light. She now regretted having done so. This joyous light struck her as a sacrilege, a miserable lie. She served Amed, seated next to his father, first. He was ashamed. He didn't dare look at his brother, who ought to have received the honor. Before starting to eat, Zahed thanked God for having given him such a courageous son. He could no longer hide his tears. Amed rose as if he wanted to speak out and admit everything. Tamara saw this. She came and held him to her. She murmured in his ear that he should say nothing: "Do it for your brother, I beg you." Amed looked at his brother. Aziz was already another person.

The meal over, the plates put away, the guests

came one by one to greet Amed, touching him, embracing him, weeping. Then they left in silence, their heads lowered as if there were nothing more to say or do. Tamara doused the garland of little lights, and the yellowish glow of candles reasserted itself in the house that seemed, suddenly, to lack air.

The two brothers climbed up to their room earlier than usual. Aziz stood before the window for a long time, studying the stars in the sky.

It was just before noon when the noise of the jeep tore the day in half. Zahed had not gone to work in the fields, and had given his two employees the day off. He, Tamara, and the two boys fixed their eyes on the horizon, incapable of doing anything else. All four waited in silence, sitting on the threshold of their house. As soon as the jeep braked in a cloud of dust, they all rose, but without taking a single step toward Soulayed. He walked toward them slowly. He was not alone. A man dragged his feet behind Soulayed, neither young nor old. He carried an old leather bag over his shoulder. Soulayed didn't give them the man's name. He just declared that the man was the "expert." He had glassy eyes and gave off a sour odor of sweat. Zahed asked Tamara and Aziz to go and wait in the house. They obeyed, reluctantly. The expert approached Amed with a smile.

"Is everything good?"

"I'm good."

"You're not very big. How old are you?"

"I'm nine."

The two men moved toward the toolshed, accompanied by Amed and his father. Amed gave the key to Zahed, who opened the padlock. Then he propped the door wide open with a plank of wood. The day projected a tunnel of light that formed a golden rectangle at the back of the shed. Soulayed asked Zahed to hand the belt to the expert, who gave it a quick examination. Satisfied, he showed Amed a little plastic-coated box that he pulled from his bag. The expert asked Amed if he knew what it was.

"No, I don't know," Amed replied timidly.

"It's a detonator. You understand?" the expert asked, looking into Amed's eyes.

"I think so."

"When the moment comes, you just have to press here."

"All right."

"You understand?"

"Yes."

"May God bless you!"

The expert attached the little box to the belt with a yellow wire.

"There's a second wire. Look at it carefully. It's red. Do you see it?"

"Yes, I see it."

"That one, we'll attach later."

"Don't worry, Amed. I'll take care of that," added Soulayed, who was standing behind him. "I'll do it just before you go up the mountain."

Soulayed said a few words to Zahed that Amed didn't understand. He then left the shed and came back a minute later, holding a camera.

"Take off your shirt," the expert instructed Amed, who obeyed, taken aback by his stern tone.

Then the expert held the belt out.

"Here, put it on."

"Why?" Amed asked nervously.

"For the photo," Soulayed explained. "Go and stand near the wall. Hold yourself straight. Turn toward the light. That's it. Don't lower your head."

Blinded and dizzy, Amed began to tremble.

"What's wrong?" shouted Soulayed. "Look at us! Think of our enemies! Think of what they did to your grandparents!"

Amed couldn't think of anything. He wanted to vomit.

"Lift your head and open your eyes! Look at your father! Don't dishonor him!"

Soulayed took a photo, then a second one.

"Think of Paradise."

Amed forced himself to smile, holding back his tears.

"Be happy, be blessed, you have been chosen by God."

Soulayed took one last photo.

"Put your shirt back on. Your parents will be proud of you when they see your photo with the belt."

Zahed took his son's hand: "The moment has come to say farewell to your mother and brother."

They left the shed. Tamara was waiting with Aziz on the threshold of the house. Aziz had around his hand a handkerchief stained with blood. He quickly explained to his father that he'd just hurt himself, cutting oranges.

"Say good-bye to your brother," Zahed said to him.

"Not right away." Aziz ran back into the house and returned with a little tray on which stood a large glass.

"Look at what your brother has prepared for you," said Tamara in a hesitant voice.

"Here, drink, that way you'll leave with the taste in your mouth of the best our land produces," added Aziz.

Aziz approached his brother and let the glass fall on him. The little accident had been devised by the twins some days before. As Amed had told his mother everything in advance, Tamara knew what was going to happen. As planned, she slapped Aziz for his clumsiness. The expert began to laugh. Soulayed silenced him. He carefully removed Amed's soiled shirt to see if the belt had come in contact with the orange juice. The expert explained that there wasn't any problem: "Water, juice, or blood, it doesn't make any difference, you still have to make contact with the detonator."

"I know," said Soulayed, irritated. "You don't have to remind me."

"Go and change," Tamara said to Amed.

"I'm going with him," Aziz added at once.

The two brothers swiftly went up to their room. They took off their clothes. Aziz helped his brother free himself of the belt.

"What's all this business about the contact?"

"It's for the detonator. Look, Aziz, it's like a little box. The expert attached it to the belt just here, you see, with the yellow wire."

"And the red wire?"

"Soulayed said in the shed that he'd take care of it."

"But when?"

"When you're at the mountain."

"Is there anything else I should know?"

"No."

"Aziz . . ."

"What?"

"Don't put the dirty shirt back on!"

Once they'd finished exchanging clothes,

Aziz gave his brother a little knife that had belonged to their grandfather. He'd found it in the ruins of his house.

"Cut your left hand, don't make a mistake."

Amed made a slash at the base of his thumb.

"Here, Amed, this is for you."

"What is it?"

"You'll see, it's a letter. You'll read it after I'm dead, all right?"

"I promise."

"No, swear to me."

Amed let a little blood from his wound drop onto the envelope.

"I swear it."

With his finger he enlarged the red stain on the envelope, as if it were a seal that secured his brother's letter, at the same time making the switch irreversible. Aziz gave Amed the handkerchief that had been dipped in sheep's blood. He wrapped it around his wounded hand. Their hearts pounding, the two brothers went back downstairs.

From this point on, Aziz was Amed and Amed was Aziz.

AZIZ

"Aziz, what's wrong?"

Mikaël had to ask a third time before the student looked up and gave him an embarrassed smile.

"Nothing, sir."

"I'm not so sure."

Mikaël had picked Aziz to play the role of Sony, a child about seven years old. It was not a difficult choice. Aziz's eyes were still those of an awestruck child, alert to everything. His voice was unusually soft for a young man of twenty. Often, Mikaël had to insist that Aziz project his voice instead of keeping it to himself. His fragile and elusive presence was a good fit with the role in which he was cast.

Mikaël had written the text especially for the

students' graduation show, which would mark the end of their four years of theater training. In a few months they would all be professional actors seeking auditions to launch their careers. As time went on, Mikaël would recognize some of them in ads for beer or shampoo. A few would get small roles in television series. Most would still be working as waiters in restaurants. But the luckiest and most talented would one day catch the eye of successful directors, who would offer them major roles as leading men or beautiful ingénues.

In Mikaël's play, Sony found himself in the hands of an enemy soldier. The child had been a helpless witness of his parents' savage killing. The soldier had cut off Sony's father's hands and shot him. Then he had raped Sony's mother and had thrown her, dead, onto her husband's mutilated corpse. Disgusted by his crimes, the soldier was reluctant to get rid of Sony, who, as scene followed scene, reminded him of his own son. The play ended after the soldier asked the child to give him one good reason why he should not suffer the same fate as his parents. Sony remained silent. Other scenes, where the two enemy camps were shown to be interchangeable, made clear the play was denouncing the absurdity of war.

Mikaël had divided the class into three groups: the father, mother, and child; the enemy soldier; the chorus of enemy soldiers. They were making good progress. The students were conscientious and focused. There was no question yet of playing out the whole range of emotions, it was still too early in the rehearsal process. They had to learn to position their bodies in space, direct their gaze, control their movements, and deliver their dialogue, unrushed but with cadence. Mikaël sensed some difficulties with the rape scene, but it unfolded without too much tension. However, an almost religious feeling took hold of the entire class when the enemy soldier approached the child after killing his parents. One had to be blind not to see that this emotion came from Aziz, and not from Sony.

"Aziz, what's wrong?"

"Nothing, sir."

"I'm not so sure."

"I can't play this role."

"Why?"

Without another word, Aziz left the class.

The next day, Aziz did not show up to class. Mikaël was very upset. Two days later, he called Aziz to propose that they meet at a café near the school. Mikaël got there early and waited impatiently for his student to arrive. On the phone, Aziz had seemed uncertain. Clearly, something was troubling him. He was already half an hour late when Mikaël caught sight of the young man's silhouette through the café's wide window. His face partly hidden by a large red scarf and a hat that was too big for him, Aziz was pacing back and forth in front of the café. Mikaël went out and gestured to him.

"Why don't you come in?"

"I don't know."

"Shall we walk a little?"

"OK."

They walked together in silence for some time. Mikaël was not at ease, Aziz even less so. It was snowing lightly, one of the first snowfalls of winter. Mikaël watched the weightless flakes spinning around him. The Latin Quarter was fairly quiet, with most people hard at work in offices, boutiques, and restaurants. Mikaël loved these vacant moments when the city caught its breath before being overrun by hordes of people hurrying home.

"Why does the child have to die?"

Mikaël was so surprised by Aziz's question that for a few seconds he didn't understand its meaning.

"The child?"

"Yes. The child in your play."

"Because . . . because it's war, Aziz."

"You want to show the cruelty of war?"

"Yes, I think that's part of the purpose of my play."

"I don't want to be impolite, but I don't agree."

"Agree with what?"

"It's not enough."

"What, Aziz? Tell me."

"To show that, all those cruel things."

"You don't want the child in my play to die, is that it? But what could he do, faced with this mercenary?"

"It's not fair."

"I know. But that's what war is."

"You don't know what you're talking about!"

Aziz's cutting tone, from someone usually so reserved, left them in silence once more. The student began to walk more quickly, and Mikaël could barely keep pace. They stopped at a street corner to wait for the light to turn green. Mikaël caught his breath and despite the snow suggested they go and sit in a little park on the other side of the street. Aziz said nothing, but followed Mikaël. He cleaned the newly fallen snow off a bench, and the two sat side by side, their arms crossed over their laps. Their breath transformed itself into little clouds of white vapor that quickly dispersed in the air.

Mikaël dared not resume the discussion. He felt attacked. Why should he not have the right, as an artist, to talk about war?

Turning to ask if Aziz was cold, Mikaël saw

a tear roll slowly down Aziz's cheek, then come to a halt, frozen.

"Give my role to someone else."

"But why, Aziz? Tell me why."

"It's not fair, I already told you."

"Of course it's not fair. The audience will feel that just like you do, and that's what I'm aiming for. I can see that you're upset. Tell me, Aziz, what happened at the last rehearsal?"

"My name is not really Aziz."

"What do you mean?"

"Amed. That's what I was called before."

"Before what?"

The daylight dimmed, and a few neon signs lit up tentatively. Since they'd left the little park, Aziz had told Mikaël the story of his childhood in one breath, his words following the rhythm of his strides. They walked through the city for a long time without quite knowing where their steps were leading them. The snow was still falling, and it gave Aziz's account a layer of protection, distancing it in space and time, lending it the texture of a fragile dream about to fade away.

"What happened after you changed places?"

"I'd sworn to my brother that I'd wait until he was dead before reading his letter. That's what I did, I waited. And that's what we did, my parents and I, we waited for my brother's death, silenced by our torment, as if we were waiting for rain or for morning to come. Two days later we had to welcome Soulayed's return as if it were a happy event. He got out of his jeep with a large package wrapped in newspapers. We all knew what it was. We sat down in the house's big room. My mother prepared tea, but no one touched it except Soulayed. We waited for him to speak, waited with our hearts in our mouths for him to tell us what had happened on the other side of the mountain. 'Your house has given our people a martyr,' Soulayed began in a ceremonious voice. 'May God bless you! Amed is now in Paradise. He has never been so happy. His happiness is eternal. Rejoice! Yes, I know your pain at having lost a son, but rejoice, lift your heads and be proud. And you,' said Soulayed, turning to me, 'cry no more, your brother is with you, do you not feel it? He has never been so close to you, never. Before the mountain, before leaving me, he told me again of all the love he had for you and your parents. Be happy and blessed.' Soulayed was silent a moment, then finished his tea. We didn't dare question him. My mother offered him more tea. He pretended he hadn't heard, and spoke again in a whisper. 'You will not hear any talk of Amed's mission from those people, that I guarantee. They are too ashamed of their defeat. Amed's deed was extraordinary. Yes, I tell you, he achieved the goal with which we entrusted him with rare efficacy. God guided him. God guided his steps on the mountain. God gave him light in the night so he could wend his way to the warehouses full of munitions. He exploded everything.' Soulayed's face then cracked open with a wide smile. His teeth gleamed with an immaculate whiteness through the dark smudge of his beard. His body was suddenly animated by new energy. He seemed taller, stronger, and he rose to strip the package he'd brought with him of its wrappings. He presented his gift to my father: the framed photograph of his dead son, his son the martyr, that Soulayed had taken in the shed. He held it up, triumphant, like a trophy. My mother shot me a pleading glance. When I saw myself in the photo, I ran from the room. A few moments later I heard Soulayed's jeep start up. Leaning from my bedroom window, I watched it drive away, hoping never again to hear its noise floating over the orange grove."

Aziz undid his coat, plunged a hand inside, and took out a folded envelope.

"Here's the letter from my brother."

The envelope was yellowed and crumpled. Unfolding it, Mikaël saw a brown stain from Amed's blood before he became Aziz. He felt an emotion that troubled him deeply. He felt that by touching and holding this envelope he was participating in the story of the two brothers. As if a fragment of their past had survived and materialized on another planet. He opened the envelope. Inside he found a short letter, written in what looked like Arabic.

"Can you translate it for me?"

Aziz read him the letter, translating as he went along. After a while, Mikaël noticed that Aziz was no longer reading. He knew it by heart, and Mikaël realized that Aziz must have recited this letter thousands of times, like a prayer.

Amed,

When I was in the hospital in the big city, I met a little girl who was our age. She was lying in the bed next to mine. I liked her a lot. Her name was Naliffa. While I slept, she heard a conversation. The doctor told Father that I would never get better. Something was rotting away inside me. No one on earth could stop this rotting. Naliffa told me everything before leaving the hospital. I thought she was brave. She herself knew what was going to happen to her. Because she, too, was very sick. She told me that I ought to know. I wanted you to know also. But not before I left for the mountain. Because if you'd known, you wouldn't have let me go. I know you well, you'd never have agreed to the switch. But thanks to you, I will know a glorious death. I won't suffer, and when you read this letter, I'll be in Paradise. You see, I'm not as brave as you think.

Aziz

Mikaël was shaken. The child who had written this farewell letter had been nine years old, the one to whom it was addressed the same age. Mikaël could see how war wiped away the frontiers between the world of adults and that of children. He gave the letter back to Aziz, unable to say a word.

The two men resumed their walk through

the city. The little Chinese neighborhood they were now passing through had been transfigured by the snow. The shops cast a reddish glow upon the men.

"My brother didn't know me. He was wrong about me. Even if my mother hadn't asked me, I would have made the swap. I was a coward."

Aziz quickened his pace, as if he wanted to run away from something. Surprised, Mikaël didn't know how to react to Aziz's admission. For a moment, he watched Aziz disappearing into the snow, now falling more heavily. He felt as if he had already lived this scene: watching someone pull away from him, together with his mystery.

"Aziz, wait for me! You did nothing wrong. Everything you've just told me about your childhood . . . how you must have suffered . . . this war that's still raging after so many years . . . your mother didn't want to lose both her sons . . ."

"You don't understand. I was afraid of that belt, I was afraid of Soulayed. So I lied, I pretended to be brave. I didn't want to die! Can you understand that?"

Amed walked and walked for a long time. Yet his steps only took him to the solitary rock in the orange grove. In a single leap, he jumped onto the rock, light as a bird. All around, branches heavy with shining fruit were swaying in the wind. Amed closed his eyes and picked two oranges at random. Feverish, he placed them on the rock, one to his right, one to the left. He sliced through the one on his right with his grandfather's knife. He found no seed in either half. He cut the other orange. Blood spurted from the fruit. He found nine little teeth. He held them in the palm of his hand and they began to melt like wax, burning his hand. Then he woke from his dream.

When he was not lying in his bed, Amed spent his time looking out his bedroom window. He told himself that by gazing at the horizon, he would eventually make his brother reappear, would make him return from the other side of the mountain, even in a thousand pieces. His mother knocked on his door and called for him, but he didn't answer. She came in anyway, and looked at him with all the sadness in the world.

"Eat something," Tamara begged.

"I'm not hungry."

"You're going to get sick. Do it for him, for your brother. Do you think he'd be happy to see you lying around like that in bed? So? You don't answer your mother? Talk to me, Amed. How do you think I feel? If there's anyone to blame, it's me. If there's anyone who ought to suffer, it's me. You understand, Amed? Leave all the suffering to me. And you, just go on living. I beg you, eat something and forget..."

Amed closed himself off in silence. Tamara shut the door.

The wound on his hand, though superficial, didn't heal. Amed kept opening it with his nails and making it bleed. Voices, ever more numerous, pursued him with accusations. They echoed in his head like shovel blows on stone. They mocked and sniggered for no apparent reason. He couldn't sleep unless he clutched his brother's pillow to himself. One night, he was overwhelmed by the certainty that he held Aziz's recovered body in his arms. It was such a powerful sensation that he wept for joy.

"Aziz didn't leave with the belt to blow himself up in the enemy's warehouses. No, I imagined the whole story, maybe even dreamed it," Amed repeated like a prayer as he fell sleep.

He hugged the pillow so tightly that in his sleep he thought blood was coming out of it. Disgusted, he woke with a start, throwing the pillow to the ground. Sitting up in his bed, he saw a dark form crouching at his window.

"Who's there?"

Amed heard someone breathing.

"You don't recognize me?"

"Grandfather!"

"Don't come near me. I don't want you to see me."

"Why?"

"I'm not a nice sight. Stay in your bed."

"Was that you I saw the other day in the shed?"

"That was my shadow."

"Aren't you in Paradise?"

"Not yet. I'm looking for your grandmother."

"She's not with you?"

"No, Amed. When the bomb fell, she wasn't in our bed. Our bodies were blasted in opposite directions."

"They found her in the kitchen," Amed said timidly. "She was making a cake."

"A cake?"

"Yes, that's what Mama said."

"The dogs, Amed."

"The dogs?"

"The dogs. The dogs! She must have woken in the night because she was afraid of the dogs. Our enemies, you know, just on the other side of the mountain. She always felt safe in the kitchen."

"You may be right."

"Listen to me, Amed. You had no right to take your brother's place."

"I didn't want to. My mother made me do it."

"You disobeyed your father. You committed a grave sin."

"But Grandfather, Aziz was sick, and . . ."

"I know, I know all that! But you defied God."

"No!"

"You defied him, Amed! That's why your grandmother and I have been separated. It's your fault that I'm living a thousand deaths. It's your fault that your grandmother hasn't found the way to Paradise."

"No!"

"We are wandering in endless darkness. I won't find your grandmother again until you avenge our deaths with your own blood. You, too, must avenge us. Your brother's blood is not enough."

"No!"

"Avenge us, or your grandmother and I will wander the world of the dead until the end of time."

"No, I don't want to! Leave me alone, Grand-father!"

"I didn't want to subject you to this, but now I have no choice. I'm leaving the shadows so you can see me. Look, Amed, see what the dogs did to me, see what is left of my body, my face. I don't even have eyes. Look at the mouth that's speaking to you, it's now just a bleeding wound. Look!"

Then Amed saw a huge mouth well up with blood and move toward him.

"Thief! Thief!

"I'm going to denounce you!

"You've stolen your brother's life!

"You've chopped his body into pieces!

"You've hidden it inside your pillow!"

That night, Amed's horrified cries woke Zahed and Tamara. When they came into his room, the child was standing on his bed, screaming with fear, and pointing his finger at the window. He'd bitten his wounded hand, and had smeared blood on his face. He kept saying that Dôdi's big mouth had wanted to eat him.

At dawn, Zahed borrowed his neighbor's truck. Something had to be done. Amed was delirious and burning with fever. Since his brother's death, he'd not stopped losing weight, and was becoming skeletal. Tamara wrapped him in a blanket and climbed with him into the truck. She herself seemed feverish and couldn't hold back her tears. A few months earlier, Zahed had rented a car to take Aziz to the hospital. Driving to the big city again this morning, he thought he was transporting the same son. He didn't suspect that this time it was, in fact, Amed that his wife was holding in her arms. They passed through several villages disfigured by recent bombings. Suddenly, Zahed stopped the truck.

"The doctor warned us. This is the end, Tamara."

"No, it's not possible!"

"We have to let him die in peace. There's no point in taking him there. It will be worse for him. And for us. Listen, we should go back home."

"I beg you, Zahed, we must take him to the hospital."

"The roads aren't safe anymore. You know that. It's become more dangerous of late. And what will that change, in any case? For me, Aziz is already..."

"You have no heart!"

Tamara was on the verge of revealing to her husband that the two brothers had traded places. But Zahed continued toward the big city.

At the hospital, when he saw his father's face bent over his own, Amed realized that something strange had happened. He'd never seen his father smiling so gently. Zahed was not the same man.

His mother explained to Amed what had occurred during the days he was delirious. The doctor had done tests, thinking Amed was Aziz. As he and his mother would have expected, there was no more sign of cancer. For the doctor who had treated his brother, it was a true miracle. He saw no other explanation for this surprising cure. It was a miracle that filled Zahed with joy, and his wife with anguish.

Back at home, Zahed told everyone he saw that his prayers had been answered: God had cured his sick child. He went to the child, touched Amed as though to reassure himself that the boy was truly alive, held him in his arms, said over and over again that his son's sacrifice was not in vain, God had rewarded him by healing his brother.

Amed was ashamed, terrified even.

A short time later, there was a period of calm in the region. The bombings almost stopped. Harvest time drew near and Zahed hired a dozen employees to help in the orange grove. The baskets of oranges piled up in the little warehouse, and Zahed decided to organize a great celebration in honor of Amed, his dead son and martyr, and Aziz, his other son, saved by God. And so it came to pass that people were invited to mark the end of the harvest that year.

Many people came. All the employees, members of their families, neighbors. Zahed also invited Kamal, Halim's father, and, of course, Soulayed. Tamara decorated the house and women from nearby came to help her prepare many dishes. Amed got new clothes. In the central room, the large photo of the martyred son was weighted with garlands. Lanterns were lit before it. Amed couldn't look. He lowered his head every time he passed before it. That photo was a lie. There had never been so many people in the house. People talked as if they were happy. This noisy happiness was also a lie. Before Tamara served the meal, Zahed insisted on leading everyone to the site of his parents' ruined house. With an energy intensified by all his listeners, he spoke of that fateful night. He described the deafening noise of the bomb, the horrible odor that followed, the debris, the mangled bodies of his poor parents. People cursed the enemies, turning toward the mountain. Just then two hands pressed down on Amed's shoulders. When he turned, Soulayed's beaming smile filled him with fear.

"How are you?"

Amed couldn't answer.

"Have you lost your tongue?"

Words stuck in Amed's throat.

"Are you Amed or Aziz? It's strange. I can never remember. The one who came with me, which one was he?"

Amed knew he was lying, or playing at not being able to remember. Everyone now knew the name of the dead martyr. Everyone had pronounced it dozens of times since the start of the celebration. It was his own name.

Amed went back to the house without saying a word to Soulayed. After the meal, Zahed rose, told everyone to be silent, and asked Kamal to address the guests. He stood in his turn, and spoke of the sacrifice of his only son, Halim. In just a few months, Kamal had aged greatly. His voice trembled, his words dropped from his mouth like tired fruit. He claimed to be the happiest of fathers. His son was in Paradise. Then Zahed gave the floor to Soulayed. His noble stature imposed a respectful silence.

"The harvest gladdens hope, and hope relies on a gaze that has no fear of seeing the truth, said our great poet, Nahal."

It was with this sentence that Soulayed addressed the people. Amed would never forget it, and afterward he repeated it often to himself. It seemed to him at once luminous and blinding, like an obsessive mystery. He was certain that Soulayed had spoken it just for him. That was an illusion. Soulayed's truth had nothing to do with his own, but he was too young to understand that clearly.

"The gaze is like a bird, it needs wings to stay aloft. Otherwise it falls to the ground," Soulayed went on. "We must never lower our eyes before the enemy. Never. Our hatred and our courage are wings that bear our gaze beyond the mountain, beyond the lie on which the dogs feed. Kamal and Zahed have understood. And their sons as well."

Soulayed then positioned himself in front of the photo of the martyr of the house, this photo that threw back to Amed his own image, and spoke of his brother's courage, of the beauty of his sacrifice. He spoke for a long time. His sentences bent around, returned to their starting place, launched themselves again with even greater force. Soulayed seemed unstoppable. All the guests drank in his words without daring to make the slightest movement. After a while, Amed realized that he was no longer listening. He stared at Soulayed's lips. They had detached themselves from his bearded face, and were projecting into the large room words that in the end had no meaning. They had become noise. Soulayed's words exploded in the air like fragile little bombs that left behind them trails of silence.

Amed went near. He moved so close that Soulayed stopped talking. He leaned over and lifted Amed into his arms. He looked at him with surprise. Amed suddenly felt very sick. As if an animal were trying to make its way out of his belly. And then he saw something in Soulayed's mouth. In his large open mouth, right in front of his eyes. Something he saw without seeing it.

"What, Aziz, what did you see in Soulayed's mouth?"

Aziz looked into Mikaël's eyes for the first time since they'd met that day.

"I don't know how to explain it to you, sir, I just can't."

"A vision? You had a vision?"

"Maybe. Yes, like a vision. But not with pictures. It was more like an odor . . ."

"An odor that you saw?"

"I don't know, sir. But it was something upsetting that had just entered my heart . . . like a premonition . . ."

"That came from his mouth?"

"Yes. That's it."

"A premonition of what?"

"Something terrible had happened, and it

had to do with my brother. And that, that thing, was there in Soulayed's mouth. It lurked there like a memory or a sensation. . . . I . . . I realize, talking to you, that this doesn't really make any sense."

"No, on the contrary, Aziz. Go on. Please. What happened next?"

"I started to shake. My body rocked with spasms. Soulayed held me against him and enclosed me in his arms. The pain in my stomach had changed. I mean, it was no longer pain, but a force that had to come out of me. I freed myself from Soulayed's grip, and ran to the photo. I smashed the glass with my fist and I tore the photo into two pieces. Then I started to shout in front of all my father's guests: 'That's me in the photo, me, Amed! There was never any miracle, the one who left was Aziz!' My father grabbed me by the neck with one hand, lifted me up and threw me against the wall. I lost consciousness. When I came to, I was lying in my bed. My mother was bent over, her face propped against the window of the room. I called to her. She turned toward me. I almost didn't recognize her. Her face was swollen. There were big black rings around her eyes. Dried blood on her nose. She told me, speaking with great difficulty, that I could no longer live in that house. I had become the son of no one."

"You had to leave your family?"

"Yes. I went to live with my father's cousin in the big city. I stayed there for several months. I was badly treated. I had dishonored my family. I did not deserve the food I was given. I was barely tolerated. I wanted to see my mother. I had no news from her. My father had forbidden her from seeing me. Then, one day, my father's cousin told me I was going to leave for America. I didn't believe him. But it was the truth. I learned that my mother, with the help of her sister, had arranged everything so that I would leave the country. I arrived on a boat with dozens of other refugees. I went to live with my aunt Dalimah. She'd lost the child she was carrying. I cried when I saw her. She looked like my mother. I couldn't stop crying."

Aziz went quiet, his eyes on his cup of coffee. Mikaël didn't dare break the silence. He raised his head to look out the wide window of the restaurant where they had taken refuge after their long walk. Night was falling fast. Mikaël could see the river far off, slipping into a bluish light. It was now snowing softly, a few lost flakes sparkling under the streetlights.

"Would you rather I called you Aziz or Amed?"

"You can keep calling me Aziz."

"Are you still cold?"

"No."

Mikaël asked for the bill, and after he had paid they left the restaurant. The sidewalks, the streets, the passersby, the roofs of parked cars, all were white, covered in spotless snow. Before leaving him in front of a subway station, Mikaël asked Aziz if he would be returning to class.

"And the child in the play?" replied Aziz.

"Don't be afraid. Sony isn't going to die."

Aziz went back to acting class. Mikaël was relieved, and at the same time perceived Aziz's return as an added responsibility. He had promised Aziz that Sony wouldn't die. For that, he had to rewrite the scene where the mercenary asked the child to give him a valid reason for letting him live. How to change that ending? Where to find the words that would touch this soldier's heart, debased by war, despairing and dehumanized? After hesitating for a while, Mikaël found the courage to ask Aziz to relate the story of his childhood, the story he'd told Mikaël as they walked. He didn't see what else he could do. Aziz's words, even improvised, would sound more authentic, truer than anything he could write for this scene. He was sure of it. He told himself that if the soldier heard the story of the explosives belt worn by a small sick child—the story of the twin brothers who traded places, which was not theater because it had really happened—and thought about his own son while listening to this story, about his son who looked so much like the little boy recounting this searing story as if it were a memory, there would then be a chance he wouldn't shoot Sony down like a dog.

"I couldn't," Aziz replied at once.

"You'll do it in your own words, very simply. Just the basics. It will take only a few minutes."

"I can't do that, sir."

"Do you want to think about it?"

"That's not necessary."

"I could help you."

"I couldn't!" Aziz cried, in a way that ended the discussion.

"I shouldn't have asked that of you. Please forgive me. Don't worry, I'll find a solution. Sony won't die. See you tomorrow, Aziz."

Aziz left without saying good-bye.

Mikaël had been rehearsing that day in the school auditorium, a flexible space that could accommodate a hundred spectators. The scenery, lighting, and costumes were conceived and executed by students in theater design, whom Mikaël supervised in collaboration with his colleagues. The class had just rehearsed the play on the set for the first time, and the day had been rather arduous. The choral sections were too slow, and a good half of Mikaël's lighting cues had to be reworked.

After Aziz left, Mikaël stayed by himself for a long while, in the middle of the set. The entire playing space was a Plexiglas floor covered in sand. About fifteen lights had been installed under this floor. The light shone from below, illuminating the layer of sand, rendering it burning hot or cold, depending on the scene. Dawn and twilight were evoked through these desert ambiences. In the course of the action, paths of light appeared in the sand, disturbed by the movements of the group. The floor was transformed into a luminous canvas, conveying to the public its cruel mystery or signs of hope.

Sitting in the sand, swathed in shadow, Mikaël was haunted by the mercenary he'd created. Was he not simply a monster? Mikaël wasn't naive. He hadn't written this text just to make his students think. He was asking himself the same questions about evil. It was too easy to accuse those who committed war crimes of being assassins or wild beasts. Especially when those who judged them lived far from the circumstances that had provoked the conflicts, whose origins were lost in the vortex of history. What would he have done in a comparable situation? Would he, like millions of other men, have been capable of fighting for an idea, a scrap of earth, a border, or even oil? Would he, too, have been conditioned to kill innocents, women and children? Or would he have had the courage, even if it meant risking his life, to refuse the order to shoot down defenseless people with a burst of machine gun fire?

"I didn't tell you everything, sir."

Mikaël gave a start. Lost in his thoughts, he hadn't noticed Aziz returning to the hall. Mikaël made out his silhouette among the rows of seats.

"I can't see you very well. Turn on the console near you."

For rehearsals, they placed a theater console in the center of the hall. It was more practical for adjusting the lighting and music cues. When

Aziz turned on the console, the stage floor lit up for a moment, dazzling Mikaël.

"It's beautiful!"

"What, Aziz?"

"The set. That light coming through the sand. It's like it's raining in reverse."

"Yes, a rain of light rising from the ground. That's it exactly."

Aziz repeated, "I didn't tell you everything, sir."

"About what?"

"About Soulayed."

"What do you mean?"

"The thing I saw in his mouth, you remember?"

"You want to talk about your premonition?"

"Yes, that thing . . . it was a lie."

"Come here. Come up on the stage."

Aziz came to sit in the sand. His face, transformed by the lighting, seemed older, harder.

"Soulayed was just a liar, sir. He lied to us the day he took my brother and me away in the jeep."

"What do you mean?"

"He told us the mountain was mined, he told us that God had guided our steps that day. It was a lie. There never were any mines on that mountain. Nor had God broken our kite string. It was only the wind. And what we saw on the other side of the mountain was not military warehouses. It was a refugee camp. Soulayed manipulated our father. He manipulated us all."

"That's horrible."

"Yes, it's horrible."

"I'm sorry, Aziz."

"Soulayed did nothing but lie to us, sir. Because of him, Paradise is a field of ruins and my brother is a murderer."

"Don't say that, your brother was only a child."

"I have the right to say it."

"Don't accuse him of having been a murderer. That is incomprehensible."

"I learned many things thanks to Dalimah's husband. My father had told us over and over, with contempt, that our aunt had married an enemy. At first, I feared the man. I couldn't help it. I had no choice, though, but to go and live in his house. And I was also ashamed. After all, if I'd been the one to leave with the belt, I could have killed his relatives or neighbors. I imagined so many terrifying things. In time,

I realized that my uncle was not a dog, as my father had said, but rather a good man who had fled his country because he could no longer endure the bombs and the attacks, the massacres and the lies. When I announced that I wanted to become an actor, my aunt was agreeable, but he wasn't. He tried to talk me out of it. He wanted me to become an engineer like him. He told me that with my accent, no one would give me a role. That I wouldn't be able to work in my new country. That I was too different. I insisted. I said to him, 'But Uncle Mani, that's what I want to do most in the world. I'm going to work hard and, you'll see, I'm going to succeed. And no one, no one will be able to tell where I come from, no one.' He didn't want to listen. So I talked to him about voices and stars."

"Voices and stars?"

"Don't think I'm crazy, sir. But every night I look at the sky and I think of my brother. I search for him in the sky."

"And have you found him?"

"No. My brother has disappeared from the sky. But I can't help myself. I keep searching."

Aziz took a bit of sand and watched it run

slowly down through his raised fist. The grains glimmered when struck by a ray of light.

"I told my Uncle Mani that I would die if I didn't become an actor."

"You really told him that?"

"Yes."

"That was perhaps a bit much. How old were you?"

"I'd just turned fourteen."

"And you already knew you wanted to become an actor?"

"Yes."

"And the voices? You talked to your uncle about the voices you heard, those of Halim and your grandfather, didn't you?"

"No, they disappeared when I arrived here. But others took their place. Many others. It's those I mentioned to my uncle. I said to him, 'Uncle Mani, don't tell Aunt Dalimah, but I hear voices. As if they were sleeping in the sky and my gaze brought them out of their slumber. They whisper, murmur, fill my head with their suffering. They're as numberless as the stars that make holes in the night. When I close my eyes, the voices light up in my head.' My uncle said I had too much imagination. All that would disappear when I had a good job, when I found the woman of my life, and when I had children in my turn."

"And?"

"I insisted. I told him that I felt as if dozens of people were living inside my head. 'Uncle Mani, maybe you're right and I have too much imagination. But how can I have less? It's as if I were always carrying around a little town inside me. I hear children playing, laughing, sometimes singing, and then there you are, I don't know why, they start to cry. After that I hear other voices, women and men the age of my parents, and others with the tired voices of older people, and all those voices panicking, lamenting, moaning, and crying with rage in a single howl. And you know what I think, Uncle Mani? All those voices, they want to be heard, and not just as ghosts in my head. If I become an actor, I'll be able to bring them into the world, give voice to them. Give voice, Uncle Mani, do you understand? A voice that everyone will be able to hear, with real words and real sentences. Otherwise they'll dwindle away inside me and I will become a ghost.'"

"Aziz, you really do have a lot of imagination. You told your uncle that?"

"Of course, sir. I had no choice."

"Why?"

"Because it was the truth."

"And how did your uncle react?"

"With another truth. Uncle Mani said to me: 'My dear Aziz, I see what you're trying to say. Yes, now I see it. Those voices you've just been describing to me, I can guess where they come from. Not just your head, I'm afraid. I think it's time I told you the truth about your brother. I never knew him. All I know about him, I've learned from your aunt Dalimah and from you. But I want you to know that for me, you are Amed and you are Aziz. You are both. Don't seek your brother any longer, because he is in your heart.' Then my uncle took my hand and held it in his own. 'Listen to me, Aziz, I have verified everything you've told me about Soulayed. I've talked to important people I trust. I've written to others. I've also searched through

the newspapers from those days. I still have a lot
of contacts back home, especially journalists.
I can assure you of one thing: there never were
mines on the mountain. Everything Soulayed
told you was false. Your brother never went to the
other side of the mountain. That was not his mission. There was no military camp to blow up. On
the other side of the mountain there was just a
poor refugee camp. The day they took away your
brother, they went south, in the same direction
they'd taken Halim. No one will ever know what
they really told your brother before abandoning
him to his fate. He must have crossed the frontier through a secret tunnel. I can't confirm it to
you. But what is certain, and nothing can erase
the history of our countries, is how your brother
died. He blew himself up, surrounded by a hundred children. Children, Aziz, children your age.
There were dozens dead and as many wounded,
seriously maimed. Those children were participating in a kite-flying competition. They'd
been brought together beforehand in a school
where they were attending a puppet show. I had
no intention of revealing that to you today. I've
talked about it often with your aunt Dalimah.

We knew that one day or another, you'd learn about it. I was amazed at first that you'd not been told about what happened when you were still back there. I imagine they did everything they could to hide this information from you. A little while ago, when you spoke to me about the voices you were hearing, I couldn't help thinking about those sacrificed children and their parents' wrenching anguish. I think you are bearing within yourself their grief for all those dead children. I think that's what you're hearing and that's what is making you suffer. It's perhaps your brother's last message, sent when he activated the detonator. Not everything can be explained. Not even war, you can't explain it when it kills children.' That's what my uncle revealed to me that day."

Aziz got up and kicked at the sand. A cloud of dust and light rose from the floor, filling the stage.

"My brother was a murderer. I can't tell his story the way you want. It wouldn't help anything. It would save no one, certainly not a child. Find something else for the scene."

Mikaël didn't know how to answer. Words caught in his throat.

"My brother is a murderer of children, sir!"

Aziz stood in front of Mikaël as if waiting for something. Mikaël observed him for a moment. With the scattered dust, the space around his body had taken on a porous, evanescent cast. Mikaël stood as well, wanting to take Aziz in his arms, to embrace him. He should have done so. Aziz just needed to be comforted.

Instead, Mikaël insisted that Aziz reverse his decision. He had to tell his story. It was the best solution. His brother's suicide attack, whether it took place in a school full of children or in a military camp, changed nothing where war's logic was concerned. In both cases, it was a matter of destroying the enemy and its means to attack and to defend itself. Mikaël heard himself uttering these words, and he found himself hateful. He couldn't think clearly, his reasoning tied him up in knots, and his arguments rang false. There was a difference between killing innocent children and blowing up military warehouses.

Anyone could see it. But without being aware, Mikaël was placing himself in the position of the mercenary character he'd created. What was there in Aziz's story that would touch him? What would persuade him to spare the child? Why would a man conditioned to kill listen to this story about a switch between twin brothers?

One question followed another and Mikaël feared that every possible answer would turn out to be another illusion. His play now struck him as pretentious and vain. He fought against the fear that his entire theatrical project would collapse like a house of cards before Aziz's story and this undeniable fact: his brother, a nine-year-old child, blew himself up surrounded by children his own age.

Mikaël went to turn off the console and turned on the house lights. He could no longer bear this lighting, shot through with shadows. He asked Aziz to come and sit in a seat next to him. For a long time they stared into the void in front of them, the great gaping stage mouth with its potential for lies and truth.

"Why did he agree to carry out such an

unthinkable act? That's the question you must have asked yourself hundreds of times. Am I right?"

Aziz stared straight ahead. Mikaël waited a moment for him to reply. Aziz seemed absent.

"You're not fair when you accuse your brother of being a murderer. How can you know what was going on in his heart when he saw what was lying in wait for him? He was deceived until the very last moment. I don't know, perhaps he was drugged..."

"You don't know what you're talking about, sir."

"You're right, I know nothing. I dared to write a play about war in complete ignorance of what it involves, of what it provokes. What business did I have doing that?"

"I didn't want to hurt you."

"But you did."

"I'm sorry, sir."

"Don't apologize. It's good that something can happen in life to shake us up and show us our own triviality."

"I like your text."

"Thank you, but it's still unfinished. And that's not what interests me, anyway, to know whether you like my text or not. That's not the question."

"You're angry, sir."

"Yes, I am!"

Aziz rose and made his way slowly to the exit. Mikaël did nothing to stop him.

SONY

Aziz didn't attend any more rehearsals, nor did he return phone calls from Mikaël and his friends. It was a serious offense. He was putting his training in danger and risking expulsion from the school. Two days before the opening, Mikaël had no choice but to give Aziz's lines to three different students so they wouldn't have too much to memorize in such a short time. In the final scene, the mercenary would no longer address Sony, now absent from the stage, but rather would speak directly to the public. In that way, every member of the audience would become the child. Mikaël was not happy with this solution. It didn't allow him to present a clear idea of the mercenary's decision: kill the child or let him live? The answer would hover in the minds of the spectators in abstract fashion. But Mikaël could do no better in his present state of agitation.

Aziz's absence had affected the morale of the group. The changes to the staging had unsettled the performances of some. Mikaël tried as best he could to remain calm, to not show his apprehension, to be encouraging. But he was shaken. He'd behaved badly with Aziz. In the end, he had no concrete idea of what Aziz had lived through in his country, of the torment that ate away at him when he imagined his brother's last moments. Had the boy understood what was being asked of him? Had he taken the measure of his act's barbarity? Had he been manipulated to the very last moment? Forced to perform the unthinkable? These unanswered questions robbed his text of all its pertinence, highlighting his own helplessness. His apprehension was enormous. His sadness, even more so.

One hour before the start of the play, to his astonishment, his nervousness suddenly disappeared. Perhaps he'd anesthetized himself without knowing it, to protect himself from his growing fears? And so he sat in the audience instead of in the control room as he had intended.

The show began a few minutes late, but everything went rather well for a first night. Yet he couldn't bring himself to concentrate on what he was seeing and hearing. It was as if his own text made him uneasy and ashamed. He tried to take mental notes of the performances for the actors, to give to them after the curtain call. He hadn't forgotten that this was also a pedagogical exercise. But as the evening moved on, he lost the thread of the show, his concentration came and went, and he found himself thinking of Aziz's brother. He imagined a little nine-year-old boy with a belt of explosives around his waist, hidden under his shirt. He saw him in the midst of other children who were also watching a show—not a war story like this one, but a story that was simply making them happy. He heard their laughter. Aziz's uncle had spoken of a puppet show. He'd like to know whether the little boy weighed down by explosives had, for an instant, forgotten his hand on the detonator, captivated by the puppets' behavior. To know, finally, whether the tragic destinies of Aziz and his brother might have been avoided.

As the play neared its end, Mikaël stopped paying attention to what was happening onstage, as if he were trying to escape his own text. But then the stunned silence of the actors pulled him out of his inner world. As if by magic, Aziz had appeared. He was standing stage right, wearing his winter coat, his red scarf around his neck. He had just come in from outside, you could still see a bit of snow melting on his shoulders. Mikaël sensed that the audience around him was confused. Clearly, the spectators were wondering whether or not the young man's entrance was part of the show. He stood out, dressed as he was, in that desert decor. The sand, in the course of the action, had been completely swept away. Now the entire floor was just a sheet of light, making the actors seem poetic or spectral, depending on their position. After a moment of hesitation, the play resumed, but nothing was the same. A sense of solemnity had descended on the hall, casting its ill-defined spell over both actors and spectators.

Aziz took a step.

"Listen to me, soldier. My name is Sony. I'm seven years old."

That was how he spoke to the actor who played his parents' assassin. He took another step.

"Listen to me, soldier. My name is Aziz. I'm nine years old."

He took another step.

"Listen to me, soldier. My name is Amed, I'm twenty years old. In my head there are other names and other ages, many others. He who is talking to you is never alone. He carries a little country around in his head. You've just killed my parents. You sliced my father's hands off with your big jagged knife. Then you slashed his throat. And shot him down. Your action was very precise. Wonderful. You must have had many occasions to practice this action to lend it such elegance. And you lost none of your deftness and concentration when you shot down my mother with your brand-new, beautiful machine gun. Who gave it to you? Was it a present? How you seem to love it and care for it! But your clothes are dirty and torn. Your hair is grey with dust and your hands red with blood.

Your shoulders slump and your gaze is cracked like a pebble. I'm amazed that you can ask me to tell you a story. I'm young, and in your eyes, I'm only a child. Do you need to hear a story told by a child? Maybe you don't see a child when you look at me? Or perhaps you only see your own? Because you, too, have a son. A son who looks like me. Who looks like us. Who looks like my brother."

Aziz advanced to the center of the stage. The light from the floor elongated his silhouette. He resembled a flame, ramrod straight, drawn up toward the sky. He spoke to the audience.

"How old are you? What is your name? You have the name of a father and the age of a father. But you have many other names and many other ages. I could talk to you as if you were my brother. Instead of the machine gun your hands are gripping so fiercely, you could be wearing around your waist a heavy belt of explosives. Your hand would be on the detonator and your heart would be on mine. And you would ask me to tell you a story so as not to fall asleep and let your hand, by accident, press the detonator. And I would talk to you until the end of time, that end which is sometimes so near."

Aziz took off his long scarf, then his coat. Mikaël felt as if he alone was watching Aziz, but he knew that every member of the audience was feeling the same way.

"Listen to me, soldier, even in the painful situation in which I find myself, I can still think. You tell me that you'll let me live if I give you a valid reason to spare me. If I capture your attention with a story that will free you from your hatred. I don't believe you. You don't need me to tell you a story. And you certainly don't need a reason to not shoot me down like a dog. You want to know what I'm doing now, by talking to you as if I were talking to a friend? I am mourning my father, I am mourning my mother and also all my brothers. There are thousands of them."

Amed took one more step toward the public.

"No, you don't need to have a reason or even to have right on your side to do what you think you must do. Don't look elsewhere for what is already within you. Who am I to think in your place? My clothes are dirty and torn, and my heart is shattered like a pebble. I cry tears that tear at my face. But as you can hear, my voice is calm. Better still, I have a peaceful voice. I am speaking to you with peace in my words. I am speaking to you in a voice that is seven years old, nine years old, twenty years old, a thousand years old. Do you hear me?"

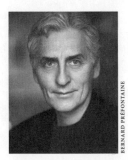

Larry Tremblay is a writer, director, actor, and Kathakali specialist. He is the author of thirty books, including two previous novels, *The Bicycle Eater* and *The Obese Christ*; one short story collection, *Piercing*; and numerous volumes of poetry. A three-time finalist for the Governor General's Award, and a finalist for numerous other international prizes, he is also the author of more than twenty plays, including *The Dragonfly of Chicoutimi*, *The Ventriloquist*, and *War Cantata*, which have been translated and produced in more than a dozen languages. Tremblay lives in Montreal.

Sheila Fischman has translated more than 150 Quebecois novels from French to English, including works by Anne Hébert, Gaétan Soucy, Jacques Poulin, André Major, Élise Turcotte, and Michel Tremblay. She has received awards for her translations and for her life's work, including the Governor General's Literary Award for Translation, the Columbia University Translation Center Award (twice), and, most recently, the Canada Council for the Arts Molson Prize. She lives in Montreal.